WHAT IF IT'S YOU

SHAUNA MCDONNELL

Blurb

My name is Ava McCann...
I'm a quirky, socially awkward hairdresser, who is
undeniably single.
I enjoy long walks to the fridge, anything from the
'90s, and nightly Netflix marathons.
Oh, and I'm completely and utterly, not in love with
my best friend, Danny.
I figure it's past time I get over my teeny tiny — okay,
huge — crush, and join the world of online dating.
But one lousy date after another has me ready to give
up on the game of love.
Could my hot-as-hell, MMA fighting best friend be
the reason Mr Right seems so far out of reach?

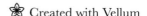 Created with Vellum

A UNICORN DOESN'T STAND AROUND WORRYING
ABOUT THE OPINIONS OF PONIES.
THEY'LL SPARKLE REGARDLESS.
BE A UNICORN!

TO BRITTNIE BECKER, THANKS FOR BEING YOU.

This book is written in British English,
spellings may differ from American English.
A lot of my characters have Irish names.
So, I've made a pronunciation chart.

CATHAL — CA-HILL

TADHG — TIGE

(LIKE TIGER WITHOUT THE R, LOL)

RIAN — REAN

AVA'S 90ish PLAYLIST

Come on Over by Christina Aguilera
Only Wanna Be with You by Hootie & The
Blowfish
Hey Mickey by Toni Basil
The Sign By Ace of Base
It's Gonna Be Me by *NSYNC
No Scrubs by TLC
The Bad Touch by Bloodhood Gang
Ironic by Alanis Morissette
Just So You Know by Jesse McCarthy
That Don't Impress Me Much by Shania Twain
(You Drive Me) Crazy by Britney Spears
Two In A Million by S Club 7

I'D DO ANYTHING FOR LOVE BY MEATLOAF

OOPS!... I DID IT AGAIN BY BRITNEY SPEARS

LIVIN' LA VIDA LOCA BY RICKY MARTIN

UP & DOWN BY VENGABOYS

C'EST LA VIE BY B*WITCHED

ICE ICE BABY BY VANILLA ICE

THE SHOOP SHOOP SONG BY CHER

SHE'S THE ONE BY ROBBIE WILLIAMS

SHE'S ELECTRIC BY OASIS

THIS KISS BY FAITH HILL

TUBTHUMPING BY CHUMBAWAMBA

'TILL I COLLAPSE BY EMINEM

EVERYBODY HURTS BY REM

TORN BY NATALIE IMBRUGLIA

BREATHLESS BY THE CORRS

ALL FOR YOU BY SISTER HAZEL

Available on Spotify

Unsolicited Penis Picture

AVA

Twenty-nine, the number of years I've had the pleasure of existing on this giant, green, and blue ball. Surprisingly, it's also the number of unwanted dick pics I've received in the past twenty-four hours.

Who doesn't love a good ole unsolicited penis picture? *Me! That's who.*

Oh, dear God, and all that's holy! This one looks like an overcooked hotdog.

Is this what my life has succumbed to — sitting at home, sans pants, on a Saturday night, scrolling through the new dating app my friend Charlotte insisted I download.

Don't get me wrong, it's a great distraction from my bubble of loneliness, but some of these guys need to brush up on their opening one-liners.

Take this one, for instance: If I was a coin, what are the chances of you giving me head?

Really, MarkyMark93? Did your mother not teach you any manners?

Swipe. Swipe. Swipe.

Oh, you're hot — heart emoji for you.

I take a large bite from my bacon double cheeseburger, and just when I think my Saturday night couldn't get any worse, tomato ketchup squirts down the front of my off-white sleep shirt.

Great, just-fucking-great.

After grabbing a napkin off the nearby coffee table, I attempt to save my now ruined tee and fail miserably. You know what, I don't give a rats arse! My vajayjay has been paging Edward Cullen for two days now. And if I want to lounge around like a big, fat, messy slob, I will.

Did you hear that, Mother Nature? You can't bring me down!

Wine, I need wine.

Clumsily, I make the necessary journey to the fridge.

If I'm going to see another male appendage tonight, I need a bottle of Aldi's most-refined-wine to get me through.

I take the wine opener from the drawer, uncork the bottle, raise it to my lips like a microphone, and sing along to the *Ladies of the 90s'* playlist that's blaring from my Bose. I am so wrapped up in my X-factor audition that I'm oblivious to the arrival of my best man friend. It isn't until he tackles the ridiculously high notes of *Come on Over* — that I'm even aware he's there.

My hand flies to my chest, adding to my dramatics, and I let out an ear-piercing scream. "Danny, are you trying to give me a heart attack? Haven't I told you — more than once — to knock before entering my lady lair?"

Without warning, he pulls the hair tie from his slightly long, brown hair and lets out a deep husky laugh. "Hello to you too, Avie. And FYI, I knocked. You just couldn't hear me over the dying cat noises you're making."

Suddenly, he shakes his head, and his hair floats around the room like Eva Longoria's in that stupid hair dye ad.

Ughh, why does he have to do that? It's highly distracting.

Also, we all know Eva spends more than €8.99 on a box dye. Seriously, who are these people trying to kid?

I don't know about most women, but there is something about the whole sexy Viking look that gets me all hot and bothered.

Danny is my very best friend in the entire world, and he's also very taken, but I can hold my chipped-nailed hands up and admit he's a sexy man-beast I'd love to taste.

He has no idea I have a teeny tiny — okay, huge — crush on him, and I'd like to keep it that way. Thank you very much.

"Danny, Danny, Danny! My singing voice could never compare to that of a dying cat. Even Queen Bey is jealous of my unique vibrato," I state, taking a bow at my excellence.

He looks at me with a raised brow. "It's certainly unique."

Like always, he opens my fridge and searches for food.

Good God, does his girlfriend never feed him?

Speaking of girlfriends...

"Where's Mandy? Didn't you guys have a date tonight?" I interrogate his ass, probably because the rest of him is lost in the confines of my refrigerator.

Finally, after some rummaging, he emerges with a

carton of milk, some cheese, and what I'm pretty sure is a *loooong* gone-off yoghurt.

"Don't ask! She has been driving me insane," he points towards my bare legs. "Nice knickers, by the way. I'm sure Wonder Woman is only delighted to have her face resting against your mammoth crotch."

Shit! I completely forgot I was doing the no-pants dance.

I pull at the hem of my shirt, trying to conceal my granny knickers — honestly, they are so big, you could use them to go camping. I'm not joking. These things would put Bridget Jones to shame.

"Shut it you, at least there are no shit stains in mine, unlike a certain someone," I taunt. "Also, mammoth? Really? My vagina's designer, thank you very much."

The mouthful of milk Danny drank — straight from the carton — sprays from his pouty lips.

He coughs, trying to catch his breath. "Okay, enough about your designer vagina. When will you let me live the skid marks down? I was five. I'm pretty sure I've learned how to wipe my arse since then."

"Really? Colour me, shocked."

I turn on my heel and exit the small kitchen — knowing full well, he will follow me into the equally small living room. Taking a seat on my two-seater couch, I cover my bare legs with the hand-knit throw

Danny's mother, Maura, made me last Christmas, and make myself comfortable.

Danny crosses the room with his usual man stride and plops himself on the couch beside me. "So, what are we watching?" His large, manly hands reach for the smart remote to my new flat-screen TV, and he kicks off his black leather boots and places his sock-covered feet on my coffee table.

"We," I gesture between us, "are not watching anything. I, on the other hand, have a penis picture to reply to, so off you pop." I wave graciously, giving the Queen of England a run for her money.

"Aww! Please don't kick me out. I don't want to go home. It's Cocks & Cocktails night at Tru bar, and Mandy's fake friends are staying the night. Please, Avie, don't subject me to all those horny women." He flashes me his big, brown, puppy dog eyes — *manipulation at its finest* — and I cave.

Well played, Danny. Well played.

"Fine, you can stay. But on one condition."

"Okay, what is it?"

With the straightest face I can muster, I bat my eyelashes. "Let me borrow your penis. I need to send some revenge dick pics."

The look on his handsome, chiselled face is highly comical. His dark brows draw together to form a deep V while his pouty lips curl up to the side, high-lighting his confusion.

"Is this a joke?" He asks, his skin looking a little paler than his usual bronzed self. "Tell me you're joking?"

Keeping my expression the same, I circle my hand in the general area of my face. "Do I look like I am joking? I've received a staggering amount of cock-tail sausage this evening. I want to return the favour. It would be the polite thing to do."

"Well, sorry to be such a disappointment to you, but under no circumstances are you photographing my dick. No-fucking-way."

He sits back into the soft leather and tears the foil lid off the yoghurt. I should tell him it's been in my fridge longer than I care to admit. But... he is with-holding his penis so he can shove it.

"Ah, why? I'm sure Pee-wee Herman loves the attention."

Holding his free hand over his penis, he looks at me as if I hurt its feelings. *Ugh, men.* "His name is Thor."

I raise my overgrown brows at him.

Note to self: Get eyebrows waxed before people start mistaking you for the dad in American Pie.

"One picture, I'm sure you have several saved on

your phone already. Isn't that what men do, compare schlong lengths over a pint of mother's milk."

"Even if I did have several photos of my Cobra Cock — and for the record, I don't — I would not, under any circumstances, be sharing them with you. I swore to myself, and to Thor, you would never see my dick again. The last time you pulled at him like a piece of chewing gum."

"We were eight, and I was curious. You can blame your ma for that one. Besides, we were too old to be sharing a bathtub. And, for the love of God, could you please stop referring to your man bits as he?"

He lifts the spoon to his mouth, opening wide, but just before it touches his lips, his nostrils flare. He sniffs once, twice, and my eyes widen. His lips twist, curling into disgust when realisation dawns.

"Ava?" He questions.

"Mm hum?" I mumble, biting back a laugh.

"How old is this yoghurt?"

I can't help it, the laughter erupts, and before I know it, I'm howling like a Lion King hyena.

He picks up the discarded lid, inspecting it closely for the expiration date. "ARE YOU TRYING TO FUCKING KILL ME? Two years, you've had this yoghurt in your fridge FOR TWO YEARS! What the hell is wrong with you?"

"Me? You're the one stealing my perishables. Maybe you'll finally learn your lesson. Stop nicking my food. Even if it's expired."

Danny's eyes glint with something I'm more than familiar with, and instantly, I know I'm in trouble. Big, stop-eye-fucking-my-best-friend, trouble. With the flick of a proverbial switch, he pounces.

"Run."

"Oh, shit!" I bounce off the chair and take off down the narrow hallway.

Smurf Gods, if you can hear me, send help!

Mount Me Mountain

DANNY

"GET OFF ME, YOU OVERGROWN MAN APE." Ava squeals from beneath me as I pin her curvy body to the carpeted floor. In what universe is straddling my gorgeous best friend a good idea? The last thing I need is to pitch a tent in my sweatpants.

Think non-sexy thoughts.

Granny's playing bingo — without their dentures.

Smelly jockstraps.

Stale gym gear.

Two-year-old cartons of mouldy yoghurt.

"Stop squirming! You tried to poison me. You're

going to eat this yoghurt, even if it's the last thing I ever witness."

Gripping her wrists with my left hand, I push them above her head. My eyes roam across her flushed face, and I suppress the throaty groan working its way to the surface as her bare legs wriggle between mine.

For years, Ava McCann had the starring role in all my teenage wet dreams. And even though we've never crossed the more-than-friends line, it doesn't mean I haven't thought about it because I have — a lot more than I care to admit.

Ava and I are just friends. I've known her my entire life, literally.

Our mothers met at a prenatal class for first-time mums, and they've been best friends ever since. Every milestone I ever reached, Ava was right there cheering me on, and vice versa.

Sleepovers, birthdays, family holidays, sneaking out, getting drunk on our mother's not-so-secret stash — we've done it all. She knows every detail of my entire life — and was there through my best and worst moments, being my best friend and biggest cheerleader.

I've always kept my untameable feelings locked away, our friendship is solid, and there's nothing I would do to jeopardise it. Ever.

Then there is Mandy, my girlfriend. She is everything Ava is not.

Don't get me wrong, they're both hot as fuck, but if you put them side by side, they are night and day.

Ava is a tiny, quirky, little unicorn with enough sass to run a small country. Mandy's tall, slim, and has a resting bitch face to match her bossy, overbearing personality.

The past few months, Mandy and I have had our problems, most of which come back to my friendship with my multi-coloured haired best friend. It doesn't matter how many times I tell her nothing is going on between Ava and me; she still chooses to make snarky, unwarranted comments.

Forcing my thoughts to the back of my mind, I dunk the spoon into the carton of Greek yoghurt on the floor beside us and gather up a more-than-generous serving. "Open wide, Avie."

She clamps her plump, peach-pink lips together and shakes her bubble-gum head from side to side.

Driving the spoon closer to her face, I make a pretend aeroplane noise as she struggles to break free. "Can you smell that?" I hover the spoon above her nostrils. "That's the mould. Two. Year. Old. Mould."

A strange noise escapes past her lips as she swallows back a gag.

"Is that your stomach churning? Is it burning your nose hair?" I won't deny the immense enjoyment I'm getting from the green hue highlighting her face.

I jiggle the spoon a little more, and a smile curls on my lips. "This is all your fault. You did this to yourself. Next time, warn a guy, and you won't end up in this predicament."

The fire builds behind her cobalt-blue eyes as determination radiates from her perfectly peach skin.

For a split second, I get momentarily distracted by her gorgeous face, but that's all she needs.

Ava shifts upwards, forcing my arms to a ninety-degree angle above her head. Thrusting her hips forward, she knocks me off balance. My hand releases her wrist, and I catch myself before I face plant the floor.

Immediately, her hands wrap around my waist as she moulds herself tightly against my chest, climbing my torso like a tree. She tucks my upper arm under her left armpit, and using all her body weight, knocks against my elbow while using her right arm to flip me onto my back.

Suddenly she has the upper hand and is straddling my waist. I can't even be mad at her for that stealthy move because I'm the one who taught it to her — in one of my female self-defence classes.

"Fuck me. Nice trap and roll escape."

"Why, thank you. I learnt from the best."

A mischievous smile reaches her eyes as she picks up the discarded carton.

My eyes widen as she tilts the container slightly.

"Don't you dare!"

My hands gravitate to her waist without thought, and I attack her sides, where she is most ticklish. The plastic container flies from her grasp, exploding and leaving us both covered in smelly lumps of cream.

AVA

What in the ever-loving fuck just happened? I could be completely crazy, but I swear, something's going on with my best friend.

Sure, we've always been close, but the whole straddling thing is not our version of normal.

Not to mention the raging hard-on that was so blatantly protruding while he was pinning me to the floor with those thighs of mass seduction.

I swear I was seconds away from calling the fire station because my ovaries spontaneously combusted.

To say I was relieved when he asked could he use

my shower — to wash away the yoghurt stuck in his thick, wavy, chin-length hair — would be a vast understatement.

I needed a minute to have a chat with myself, anyway.

Sure, I'm the queen of bad decisions, but I'm a thousand per cent confident that molesting my very handsome, very taken best friend would be the icing on the sinfully, delicious, you-can-never-eat-that cake.

Danny has always been a significant figure in my life. He was there when I took my first steps. He taught me how to ride my bike.

Danny was the guy who held my hand through my da's funeral. The one who punched Bobby Daly in the face when he took my virginity then never called me again.

Danny O'Donoghue is my constant.

That's why I never told him when my feelings for him shifted to something more than best friend status.

Losing him would never be worth the risk.

Currently, I'm trying to ignore the fact that he is very naked in my shower, but no matter how hard I try, the image of his rock-hard, semi-professional MMA body is dancing through my mind.

Bad Ava, we talked about this — no more imagining your best friend naked.

Just when I finally exorcise his highly impressive abs from my very own female spank bank, he strolls into my living room in a freaking towel.

Just. A. Towel.

Can eyes have orgasms?

Because I swear to the Lord above, that's what's happening.

The white cotton is draped low on his hips, kissing the sculpted V carved between his hip bones. I force myself to lift my gaze, only to be stunned silent by the wet, glistening ridges of his abs.

Fuck me sideways.

Danny's deep vibrato cuts through my daydream. "Ava, you're catching flies."

I'm well aware, Danny! Can you blame me? You're standing there like a half-naked, hot Viking model from that thirst trap app, also known as TikTok.

Coughing away my in-a-dazed state, I question, "Where are your clothes?"

"They're full of yoghurt. Have you anything that I can throw on? Surely, you have something that belongs to me. You've been stealing my clothes since puberty."

He calls it stealing. I call it borrowing, indefinitely.

"Umm, yeah. I'll just umm." Looking everywhere

but his tattooed torso, I rise from the chair and all but sprint down the hall.

Girl, you need to get a grip on your hormones. It's just Danny. No need to hyperventilate.

Searching through my wardrobe, I find a pair of sweats and his old University College Dublin hoodie. They might be a little snug since he's grown a helluva lot since then, but they'll have to do.

Taking a second to calm my sex-crazed libido down, I blow out a staggered breath and head back to the living room. It's okay. We are both grown-ups.

Surely, we can ignore the giant elephant in the room. *And no, I'm not referring to the trunk-shaped outline protruding from beneath his towel.*

"Here you go." I throw the clothes at him, making sure to keep a reasonable distance.

"Cheers."

Plonking myself on the couch, I pretend to flick through the recently added section on Netflix as I side-watch Danny from the corner of my eye.

He pulls on the sweats, then whips the towel away.

Oh, what a shame! Is one peak too much to ask for, geez?

Lifting the slightly damp towel to his drip-drying hair, he roughly runs it through his mane. "I need a haircut," he grumbles.

Pretending to not ogle him, I continue my search for something decent to watch. "Come by the salon sometime this week. I'll get Charlotte to squeeze you into my schedule."

"Thanks, that would be great. Mandy has been on my case for weeks. She hates my long hair."

Is she fucking blind? Who wouldn't want a man with a head of hair that could rival Charlie Hunnam?

There isn't a woman alive that wouldn't give her left nipple to ride that train to Mount Me Mountain.

Capital letters essential!

Lifting my now covered legs, Danny squeezes in beside me on the two-seater couch. "Sons of Anarchy? Haven't we watched this enough?"

"Let's just say I need my Jax Teller fix."

"Fine, you win."

"Don't I always."

Prime Piece Of Man Meat

AVA

TODAY IS THE MONDAYEST FRIDAY IN THE HISTORY OF all Fridays.

It's barely lunch, and already, I'm in dire need of a nap. Or at least four cups of coffee.

Lord knows, I'm no stranger to a busy day, but today, teenager after teenager came into the salon, all wanting sleek locks for their Senior class Debs.

Fuck me, pink. If one more person asks me for Hollywood waves, I'm slapping a bitch.

Oakhill is a small town on the Dublin-Meath border. It's not Los Angeles. Whatever happened to a good ole fashioned GHD curl? And don't get me started on the lip-fillers and lash extensions. These girls are barely eighteen, and already they're walking around like Pamela Anderson — post-Baywatch.

Somehow, I manage to squeeze in a small two-minute break between clients, so I rush to the back-room to wolf down my pre-packed sandwich.

I'm only three bites in when my closest female friend, Charlotte, interrupts my already deprived break.

"Ava, your next client is here."

I throw my head back and roll my eyes to the high heavens. "Any chance you can get her started? I'm starving. I'll only be two minutes," I beg, batting my eyes at her.

"As much as I'd love to run my fingers through Danny's hair, we both know you're the only one he allows near his luscious tresses," she quips, fanning her face for dramatic effect.

"Shit." I haven't spoken to Danny since our little roll-around-slash-not-foreplay on Saturday night. Well, that's not counting the odd, and if not slightly awkward, text messages we've exchanged over the last few days.

The tension between us rose past this-is-embar-rassing, to get-me-the-hell-out-of-this-room-before-I-curl-up-and-die. Sure, we stayed up and watched a few episodes of SOA, but as soon as I could, I high-tailed it to my bedroom, away from him and all his sexiness.

By the following morning, he was gone.

"Ava Marie McCann, care to explain why you look like you've seen the ghost of bad decisions past?"

Chewing on my slightly soggy ham and cheese sandwich, I evade her question like the goddamn boss bitch I am.

Charlie places her hand on her hip while raising her eyebrow. "Oh no, you don't. If you don't tell me what happened between you and that prime piece of man meat, I'll just ask him myself."

Spinning on her low-heeled boots — because, let's be honest, no hairdresser in their right mind would wear anything more — she heads for the door.

"Wait!" I grip her wrist and pull her back in the doorway. "I'll tell you."

Charlotte folds her arms under her D cup breasts and hits me with a look.

I'm waiting.

"Danny came over to my place last Saturday, and things got a little —"

"Frisky, steamy, naked. All three." The words fly from her mouth like a bad case of diarrhoea.

Picking up a semi-wet hair towel from the over-flowing laundry basket, I whip her with it.

"Would you shut up and just listen?"

"Sorry, sorry... please, continue."

"As I was saying, things got a little... uh, I don't know, awkward."

Her face scrunches, showing off a deep furrow in her perfectly manicured brows. "Awkward? How?"

"I don't know. We were shooting the shit like always, then he chased me down the hallway and somehow ended up straddling my waist and poking me with an impressive penis."

Pressing her plump lips together, she fights back a laugh. "I don't see what the issue is. For as long as I've known you, you've wanted that man to poke you with his penis."

I huff out a frustrated breath as my shoulders sag with deflation. "The point is Danny has a girlfriend. A very real, beautiful, curvy girlfriend. I can't compete with that, and honestly, I don't even know if I want to. Danny's great, and I love him to pieces, but dating him? I don't know. He's my best friend. If things between us didn't work, I'd lose a lifelong friendship."

Standing from my stool, I throw the rest of my half-eaten sandwich in the bin. "Besides, I could be reading into this whole situation, and then what... I tell him how I feel, and he laughs in my face. I don't think I could handle that."

"Ava, how many times do I have to tell you? You're gorgeous. I would kill to have a body like yours. If Danny can't see how beautiful you are, inside and out, well then, it's his loss."

Pulling me into her arms, she wraps me up in one of her carebear hugs. "How are things going with the dating app? Have you any potential dates lined up? It might help you take your mind off a certain sexy someone."

Stepping from her arms, I tell her about Barry. "We've been texting on and off all weekend. He wants to take me for dinner tomorrow night at Tru. I figured it was a safe place to meet him for the first time."

"I agree. You never know what kind of freaks these people are. He could be eighty-seven and living at home with his dead wife's corpse. Do you want me to come? I'll bring Tadhg. We can sit in the corner and stalk you. You know, just to make sure you're safe?"

"Ha! No, I'll be fine, everyone knows me there. If I need rescuing, I'll get Cathal to help me.

"Now, there's a man I wouldn't mind getting

underneath. He was pouring a pint for Tadhg last weekend, and the protruding veins on his forearms," she blows out a breath, "there are no words."

Throwing back my head, I laugh at the dreamy look on her face. "You're insatiable. I'm sure your boyfriend would love to hear you talking about his best friend like that."

"Hey, just cause I'm on a diet, don't mean I can't look at the menu."

Raising my brow, I give her a pointed look. "You keep telling yourself that. Now, if you'll excuse me, I have a client."

DANNY

I find myself becoming increasingly nervous as I stand in the reception area of BedHeads — the salon where Ava has worked since she was sixteen. I'd love to say I've not been avoiding her since last weekend, but that would be a blatant lie.

Saturday night, after Ava went to bed, I couldn't get the thought of her underneath me out of my head. I spent most of the night wide awake, feeling guilty. Then, when the sun started to rise, I got the hell out of dodge.

Mandy deserves better. Fuck, so does Ava. I had to put some needed distance between us.

Yet, here I am, less than a whole week later, standing in her workplace, holding a cup of her favourite unicorn hot chocolate and a box of Krispy Kreme doughnuts. I'm still not sure what I'm going to do with the growing ache I have to kiss my best friend, but for now, I'll act like the grown man I am and pack it away.

I'm in a relationship, and for the most part, Mandy makes me happy. There's plenty of words to describe me, but a cheater is not one of them.

Suddenly, the little ball of colour comes strutting across the salon — wearing skin-tight black leather pants that mould to her never-ending curves and a black cropped t-shirt that shows off the cherry blossom tattoo wrapped around her right side.

Fuck, maybe this wasn't such a great idea.

"Well, hello stranger," she sasses. She points to my hands and smiles wide. "Please tell me those are for me."

"They sure are." I pass her the cup, and she steps forward, giving me a one-armed hug. The same electric current I always feel when we touch travels down my spine. I subconsciously step back. I need to get a grip on this tiny crush before I fuck up everything.

"You're the best. Today has been a nightmare." Lifting the cup towards her lips, she blows into the small circular hole on the lid, then takes a sip. I don't miss the tiny groan she releases as the hot liquid coats her tongue — and neither does my dick.

Jesus. H. Christ! When did everything she does start to turn me on?

Ava leads me over to her section, and it takes all the strength I possess not to stare at her ass as she sways her hips with every step.

"So, what are we doing today?" She asks once I take a seat and place the box of doughnuts on the sectional. "The usual trim?"

"No, I have a fight coming up in a few weeks, so I was thinking of shaving the back and sides tight and leaving a little length on top."

"Okay, cool. The Viking Undercut will look great." Ava gets busy preparing all the equipment she needs, but I can't help noticing she seems withdrawn.

She sections off my chin-length hair and gathers the upper half into a top knot with her shaky hand.

"Are you okay?" I ask. "You seem a little off-kilter."

"I'm fine, just tired and hungry. Someone —" Ava's eyes catch mine through the giant mirror "— cut my lunch short."

"Oh, hangry, Ava. Maybe we should do this another day. I wouldn't want to lose an ear," I joke, trying to lighten the apparent tension between us. "Plus, I brought you doughnuts."

"They're the only reason I haven't scalped you." She raises the razor with an evil glint shining from her cobalt eyes.

"How about to make up for interrupting your lunch... tomorrow after your shift, I'll treat you to your favourite chicken wings?"

"As appealing as that sounds, I can't. I have a date tomorrow. Make it Sunday breakfast, and you have a deal."

A date? With who?

I try to keep my expression neutral, but on the inside, I'm burning up with jealousy — even though I know I have no right to be. Ava is beautiful, single, and free to date whoever the fuck she wants.

Do I have to like it? No, no, I do not.

Acting as casual as I can, I reply, "Sunday's good. So, a date, huh? Anyone, I know?"

She shrugs her shoulder while running the shaver through the back of my hair. "No, I don't think so. I met him on the dating app Charlotte made me join. He's from Monaghan."

She doesn't even know this chap! He could be a serial killer, for all we know.

"Where are you meeting him? I hope it's somewhere public. You never know what kind of loony bins are on those sites."

Her boisterous laugh fills the air. "Don't worry, Dad. I'm meeting him at Tru. What is wrong with everyone today? First, Charlie, and now you. I'm a big girl. I can look after myself."

I know you can, Avie. The problem is, I want to be the one who looks after you.

Woah! Where the hell did that thought come from?

Maybe her dating someone is not a bad idea. It might help me place her back in the just-my-friend zone.

"You're right. You can. Have fun on your date, and if you need anything — an escape, a ride home, someone to kick his ass — call me, okay?"

"Yes, Sir. Now, shut up and let me make you pretty."

We're Shipping You

AVA

"Mam!" I call out as I enter my childhood home with my best girlfriend, Charlotte, hot on my heels.

It's been years since I lived under my mother's roof, but nothing has changed. Everything is how it's always been; magnolia wallpaper and an old-fashioned, off-cream carpet that's older than I am. Picture frames hang proudly, highlighting childhood memories and achievements — everything from our preschool days to Suzie — my younger sister's — wedding last spring.

When our dad died almost seven years ago, ma became very sentimental, keeping everything the way it was when he was still here.

Their love was one for the ages. They met when they were kids and fell in love as teens, and I'm sure it's hard for her to let him go. I always wanted what they had — a love that lasts a lifetime.

Mam's cheery and boastful voice travels down the narrow hallway, guiding us towards the kitchen. "In here, darling."

For as long as I can remember, Friday nights have been for the girls. It's a tradition my ma started with Danny's mother, Maura, almost thirty years ago. As far as I'm aware, they've never missed a single week.

The aroma of Chinese take-out wafts throughout the house, making my stomach cry out in protest. I haven't eaten since my interrupted lunch, so it's safe to say I'd eat a horse and chase the jockey.

"Just in time," Mam greets while she plates us up some food. "Greg just dropped Suzie off, and she brought all your favourites."

"Hey, sis," Suzie raises her glass of pink gin.

"Hey!" I gaze around the room, searching for my niece and nephew. "Where are the twins?"

"With Greg. This mammy needed a night off."

Two years ago, Suzie gave birth to The Terrible

Duo, also known as Ellie and Ethan. And let's just say she has her work cut out for her. Just last week, Ellie found Greg's hair clippers and shaved the cat.

Shaved. The. Cat!

Apparently, she was trying to be just like her Auntie Ava and cut peoples hair.

I was both honoured and horrified by her dedication.

"Bring them to see me soon. I miss those little assholes."

My gaze darts towards Maura, and I smile wide. Maura O'Donoghue is the second mother I never needed but got anyway.

Her fiery, red hair matches her boss-mom personality. And with three boys — Danny, Keegan, and Kye — all eighteen months apart, how could she be any other way. Somebody had to keep them hellions on their toes.

I sink onto the barstool beside her and give her a side squeeze. "Hey, Mamma-two!"

"Hello, daughter-to-be."

"How many times do I have to tell you... I'm not marrying any of your sons?"

She laughs. "I live in hope."

Charlie plops herself down on the stool beside my ma, but her humour filled eyes look towards Maura.

"You might get your wish sooner than you think. From what I hear, Danny boy might be getting a bit of sense."

If looks could kill, six feet under, she'd be.

"Oh!" Ma freezes mid-air, hovering over her seat. "If you've got the tea, Charlie. You'd better spill it. Lord knows my daughter won't."

My eyeballs roll. "Nobody will be spilling anything. The teapot is empty. Not a drop of tea in sight."

"Hmmm…" Maura's eyebrows rise. "I don't believe you, missy. My son has been acting like someone stole his puppy all week. I presumed it had something to do with Moany Mandy, but now, I'm not so sure."

Suzie cackles. "Oh, my god! Moany Mandy!" Her hand slaps down on the kitchen island. "Does she know you call her that?"

"Of course," Maura states. "Lesson number one: never say something behind someone's back if you're not prepared to say it to their face. Danny has been with that girl for ten months now, and I swear to the lord above, she keeps getting worse. Just yesterday, she rang Danny to complain about him having Sunday dinner at my house. That boy has eaten at my table every Sunday for the last twenty-nine years. That won't change anytime soon."

Hell has no fury like an Irish mammy, especially when it comes to her son.

"He's a grown man. He has his own life." My ma interjects.

"I pushed that boy out of my hooch. The least he can do is show up for an hour once a week."

Oh, Jesus, I could have done without that visual.

"Anyway," Maura adds. "What happened between the two of you?"

If I've learned anything in the last few years, it's that these women don't quit.

"Nothing happened."

"Bullshit!" Charlie announces with a mouthful of spring rolls.

Have you ever felt the need to murder your best friend, and if so, have you any tips?

"For fuck's sake, Charlie. Would you shut up?"

"No! Everyone in this room is invested in this potential relationship. We need information."

"Yes," Ma agrees. "We're shipping you."

"HASHTAGTEAMDANNYANDAVA!" Maura raises her wine glass.

"Maura, that's not how hashtags work," Suzie

laughs. "You gotta blend their names. Like Bey-Z or Kimye."

I roll my eyes, lower my forehead, and bang my head against the countertop. Finally, I lift my head, only to find four sets of curious eyes on me.

"Jesus, you are all relentless. It was nothing," I admit. "We were just messing around, and we ended up rolling around on the floor. There may or may not have been a little straddle. I could be reading into it, but for a moment, it felt as if our just friend's line disappeared, then it was awkward as fuck. To be honest, I rather forget about it. Danny loves Mandy, and I need to accept that and move on from my stupid, teenage infatuation."

"Whatever you say, sis!"

The rest of the evening goes by without a hitch. Well, that's if you don't factor in the constant badgering from Maura and my mother. The two of them were minutes away from planning my hypothetical wedding to Danny. Three bottles of wine later, and they were naming their non-existent grandbabies.

Charlie and Suzie did nothing to deter them, only adding fuel to their bonfire. It was then I decided it was time for me to get going. I had enough of their ridiculous notions.

I need to remind myself that Danny will only ever be my best friend. We drew a line all those years ago, and I have no intention of crossing it.

Not now, nor ever. I am happy with the friend zone. I am safe there.

If there is one thing I know, it's that if I ever crossed that line and it ended badly, I wouldn't survive. I can't allow myself to fall in love with Danny O'Donoghue, because from that fall, I would never recover.

AFTER LEAVING MA'S, I DROPPED CHARLIE OFF AND came straight home to my giant empty bed and my Netflix account.

Okay, so it's Danny's account. I haven't made it to that level of adulting.

I pull back my unicorn duvet set, climb into bed with the box of doughnuts Danny brought me earlier today, and settle in.

Deciding on Schitt's Creek, I press play, open the box of Krispy Kreme's, and burst out laughing. Inside are four pastel-coloured, Swizzler themed doughnuts. I reach for my phone and shoot Danny a text.

Ava: Just opened my doughnuts! Thank you, I love them.

Danny: They're limited edition. When I saw them, I had to get them for you.

I stick a doughnut in my mouth, cross my eyes, snap a picture, and hit send.

Ava: You're the bestest friend a girl could have.

The three dots flash across the screen, then disappear. I'm halfway through the next episode when my phone pings with an incoming message.

Danny: Goodnight, Ava.

Weird.

Vitamin V

DANNY

My gloves pound against the punch bag at rapid speed.

Sweat drips down my naked back, beading in every dip and crevice.

I need this, the burn coursing through my veins.

"Left, right, jab. Left, right, jab." Over and over, rinse and repeat.

Finally, after I've exhausted myself, I drop my ass to the mat and drag my knees to my chest.

I draw in a deep breath and slowly release.

"Jesus, D. Who shat in your breakfast this morning? For a moment there, I thought you were going to barrel right through me."

Ignoring my youngest brother, Kye, I lift my water bottle to my lips and empty it in one giant gulp.

"What's wrong?" He continues. "Did Mandy cut you off again? No vitamin-V for Danny's D."

I swipe the towel across my forehead, then level him with a glare. "Do you ever shut up?"

"What's wrong? Did I hit a nerve?" He wiggles his brows, irritating me further.

Pushing myself off the mat, I shake out my arms and legs and head for the power rack.

"Ignoring me won't fix your relationship problems," he prods.

I turn on my heel, stopping abruptly. "I never said I had relationship problems."

Lifting his hand, he directs it toward my chest and pokes. "You didn't have to. It's written all over your ugly mug. What pissed Mandy off this time? Sunday dinner at Ma's, or was it Ava?"

I can't help it. My left brow twitches at the mention of Ava's name.

Unfortunately for me, Kye catches it.

"Now I'm getting somewhere."

Shaking my head, I turn, grab onto the mounted

chin-up bar attached to the power cage and start my reps.

"Come on, D. Don't leave me hanging. What did Cee-Cee do?"

For as long as I can remember, Kye has referred to Ava as Cee-Cee, a.k.a Cotton Candy. She loves that stupid nickname.

Me, not so much.

You're just jealous, asshole.

"Ava," I stress. "did nothing. Mandy is just being Mandy."

I pull up, lifting my chin above the bar and keep my elbows bent; pausing for a second, I lower myself back down. "Last weekend, I stayed the night at Ava's, and Mandy lost her shit. She says I spend too much time with Avie and that she wants me to stop seeing her. Naturally, I disagreed with her. Avie has been my best friend for twenty-nine years. Nothing will change that. So now, I'm sleeping on the fucking couch."

"Ouch! You've slept over at Cee-Cee's before. Now it's a problem?" he questions.

"She-wants-to-get-married." The sentence blurs into one word.

Kye's brow raises, and his mouth hits the gym

mat. Continuing with my chin-ups, I wait for him to comment.

"Married? As in lifetime commitment, house, and ten kids?"

I shift my body weight and move to a different handle angle, making sure to work all my back muscles evenly. "Yeah. Only she wants three kids, not ten."

"And what do you want?"

An image flashes behind my eyes, one that scares the ever-loving fuck out of me.

Ava McCann.

Up until very recently, I was content with my life.

My MMA career is finally taking off. I have a girl-friend who, for the most part, makes me happy. My family life is solid, and my little crush on my best friend is locked away safely in the never-open-this box. Or at least I thought it was.

Dropping my feet to the mat, I drag in a deep breath. I run my hands through my hair and exhale.

"Honestly, Bro, I have no idea. I never really thought about it, not until recently. Now, I'm more confused than I've ever been."

"Can I say something without you punching me in the nut sack?"

I nod, knowing well what's coming.

"Ever since we were kids, it's always been you and Cee-Cee. For the longest time, I was so jealous of you. We all adored her; You, Keegan, and me. But you, with you, it was different. You guys had this friendship that the outside world couldn't reach. Then as you both got older, I always wondered why you never made your move. What I'm trying to say is, I always thought you'd marry Cee-Cee."

Grabbing my towel and water bottle from the floor, I push back the image of Ava in a wedding dress, then head for the dressing room. I've had enough of this shit for one day. I need to sort my head out, quick.

"We're just friends. Nothing more. I'm with Mandy," I toss in Kye's direction, reminding him, and also me.

EXHAUSTED FROM TONIGHT'S WORKOUT, I DRAG myself up the staircase of my apartment complex and all but crawl to my door. Shifting my gym bag onto my back, I stick my key into the lock and twist, pushing the door open with my foot. I'm in dire need of a long, hot shower and at least a week's worth of sleep.

"Daniel?" Mandy calls out. "Is that you?"

Kicking the door closed behind me, I drop my gear bag to the floor. "Yeah, babe."

The distant clicking sound of heels-on-floorboards grows louder, and suddenly, Mandy appears. Her hand grips her waist, crunching the material of her little black dress, and her chocolate brown eyes scan me from head to toe. Judging by the disdain twisted on her pouty red lips, I'm in for it.

"Where have you been? I've been calling you all day."

"I've got a fight coming up. I've been at the gym training."

My body is aching in all the wrong places, and I'm way too tired to argue over my whereabouts. It's times like this, I wish I didn't move in with her. Don't get me wrong; the first two months were great, but ever since she brought up the 'M' word, things between us have been ropey. She wasn't impressed at my I-don't-think-we're-there-yet answer.

Since then, I've been walking on eggshells. I can't piss in peace, and no, not figuratively speaking — yesterday she watched me take a leak.

"That's not acceptable, Daniel. When I call you, you answer," she turns on her heel. "Get ready. We are meeting my friends for dinner. We can't be late," she adds, throwing the words over her shoulder.

Fuck this.

"NO!"

Okay, so I'll admit, that may have been a tad aggressive, but I'm a twenty-nine-year-old man. I can make my own plans, and the last thing I'm in the mood for is a night out.

She turns so fucking slowly, and the tension rises. "Excuse me? Did you say no?"

Her fake lashes flutter in disbelief as she stands there with a face that looks as if it's been chewing nettles.

"I don't want to go out, Mandy. I've been working all day. I'm exhausted. Can't we stay in, maybe order a takeaway?"

Her nostrils flare as she tucks her top lip between her teeth. *Oh, she's mad.*

"Working? You cannot be serious, Daniel? Fighting is a hobby, not a career. You can hardly say you've been slaving all day to put food on our table. I, on the other hand, have put in an eight-hour shift. I can still call you, come home, and be ready for a night out with our friends."

Her head bobs from left to right. "I'm certain if

Ava called, you'd be there in a heartbeat. It's a Saturday night; you can't expect me to stay at home."

There are so many things wrong with that sentence. Honestly, I don't even know where to begin.

"I was working, Mandy. I'm a personal trainer at the gym six days a week. Excuse me for chasing my dreams, too. Forgive me if I want more from life than a nine-to-five. I fight because I love it. It's a part of who I am. I'm sorry if I am so fucking bone-tired from working all day, and training all evening, that all I want to do is curl up and watch a movie with my girlfriend."

Lifting my hand, I wave towards the door. "But by all means, if you want to go out, go ahead. I am not stopping you, but I won't be joining you. I'm shattered."

That was the wrong thing to say. Before I can correct my error, she stalks toward me, closing the distance between us.

"I'm so over this. You never make any time for me. You're so busy running around after everyone else. What about me?" She stomps her foot, and I almost laugh at how childish she's behaving.

You'd swear I was out every night of the week when in reality, it's quite the opposite. I rarely see my brothers, unless it's at our da's gym. Mandy refuses to hang out with my friends, so I only see them when she's made other plans. I'm here every night. She's the one that's never home.

"You have two choices here, Daniel." She pokes me in the chest with her long nails. "Either you shower and come with me... or you pack your bags and get the hell out of my apartment. I'm sick of always being your second choice."

I blink. "Are you for real? You're kicking me out because I am too tired to go for dinner with your friends?"

I take a step back and run my hands through my hair. "What's this about? Is it because I'm not ready to marry you?"

This is a side of Mandy that, up until recently, she kept hidden. She throws down these empty threats to get her way, and frankly, I'm getting pissed off with her my-way-or-else manipulation.

"This has nothing to do with that. It's about your blatant disregard for my feelings."

"Fuck you and your feelings. I've spent the last eight months doing everything you wanted me to. I bend over backwards, trying to be the man you want me to be, and no matter what I do, it's never enough."

I reach down and pick up my gear bag from the

floor. "You hate my family. You think you're above my friends. And now, my career is only a hobby."

I turn around and pull the door open.

Mandy squeezes between me and the open doorway, blocking my exit. "Where do you think you're going?"

"I'm done. You keep trying to change me, mould me into someone I'm not. I can't keep doing this."

Refusing to move, Mandy runs her hand down my chest, stopping at the waistband of my grey tracksuit bottoms. "I'm sorry." Her voice drops to a seductive tone. "Please don't go."

I know what she's doing. It's what she always does to get her way — blinds me with the offer of sex. This time, it won't work, though.

Gently, I take hold of her wrist and remove it from my skin.

"Enough!" I hold firm. "I can't do this anymore."

I push past her. "We're finished, Mandy. I'll come by tomorrow and get the rest of my stuff."

"Fuck you, Daniel. You suck in bed, anyway."

"It's Danny!"

And as for the suck in bed comment, she wasn't thinking that ten seconds ago when she tried sticking her hand down my jocks.

Dear, Sweaty, Definitely Balding, Barry

AVA

I'VE BEEN ON SOME BIZARRE DATES IN MY LIFETIME, but this is a whole different kettle of fish.

Firstly, Barry looks nothing like his profile picture, and I do mean nothing. I was expecting a fine specimen of a man. But in fact, he is an over-aged, overweight, five-foot-three banker named Barry.

Call me crazy, but when you advertise yourself on a dating app, are you, or are you not meant to use a photo of yourself?

Naively, I thought I was meeting a Channing

Tatum look-alike. Let's just say Barry is more Donald Trump.

I know you think it can't be that bad, but trust me, it's worse.

Not only does he look like he's bathed in a bottle of Cocoa Brown tan, but his bleach blonde wig has been practically waving at me throughout the entire meal.

Look, I'm not a vain human by any standards, but I do have standards.

And Barry, dear, sweaty, definitely balding, Barry, does not meet them.

Secondly, even if I were to get past him lying about, um, everything. I couldn't possibly get past his ever-present need to fist pump me after every single sentence.

Every. Single. Sentence.

Honestly, this date could not be going worse than it is.

"So, Ava. On your profile, it states you are a hair-stylist. How did that come about?"

Batman, Superman, Wonder Woman! If any of you can hear me, please, for the love of my sanity, save me.

Why did I let Charlotte talk me into doing this? Would it be rude if I just excuse myself to go to the bathroom, then never return?

Swallowing down the piece of bread roll I just bit into, I reply honestly, "Erm, I've always been a creative person, and I love how you can change a person's whole appearance with just a simple cut or colour change. When I was a kid, my grandmother always said, invest in your hair. It's the crown you never take off. And I guess it kind of stuck with me because I've been obsessed with hairdressing ever since."

"That's an awesome story." He raises his closed fisted hand until it's hanging awkwardly in the air, above our food.

"Gimme some," he wiggles his suspended knuckles in my face.

Mortified, I quickly bump my fist against his, then silently will the ground to open up and swallow me whole. If only I were so lucky, but unfortunately, I'm not.

Barry rears his arm back, spreading his fingers wide and shouts 'boom' for the entire restaurant-slash-bar to hear.

Embarrassed doesn't even begin to cover what I'm feeling right now. My cheeks are so hot; I could prob-ably turn my medium rare steak into well done with just a look.

My eyes involuntarily glance around the room as I

plead with Jesus that nobody saw that little display. Suddenly, Cathal Daly, the sexy, hot-forearmed barman, locks his stunning green eyes on mine.

Judging by the sly grin curled around his lips, he has witnessed every painfully embarrassing moment.

Picking up my glass of chilled Rosé, I take a small sip and try to ignore the laughter lines around Cathal's eyes. *Asshole.*

Looking back at my date, I ask, "What about you? Did you always want to be a bank manager?"

"Yes, numbers are a fascinating thing. Why would I want to be anything else? Am I right?"

Please don't. Oh, too late.

Barry's hand lingers in the air, ready and waiting for me to blow it up.

Just then, Cathal emerges. "Good evening, sorry to interrupt your meal, but Ava," his emerald eyes home in on mine. "Charlie is on the office landline. Sounds like an emergency." He sends me a look, eyes wides and brows raised, and I hear him loud and clear.

Just go with it.

Gathering my things, I pull out a fifty euro note from my purse and place it on the table. "I'm so, so sorry, Barry, I had a lovely time, but I need to —"

"Go. It's okay. Thank you for gracing me with your beauty. I will call you during the week."

Please don't.

Giving 'Here Comes the Boom' Barry one final head nod, I follow Cathal across the bar, through a side door that reads 'Staff Only'.

"Thanks for... umm, the help with," I motion in the general direction in which we came.

"Don't worry about it. You're not the first girl I've rescued from a blind date fail, and I doubt you'll be the last. However, you are the first one I've witnessed getting fist-pumped every five seconds. So, thank you for providing me with a night of entertainment."

"Glad I could provide you with such a humorous shift."

"So, I take it your online dating is going well?" he smiles.

"Oh, yeah! I seem to be getting the full experience."

"Sarcasm noted."

We come to a halt outside a small office, and Cathal opens the door and waves for me to enter. "Don't worry. You can hide out here until he leaves."

Looking up, I take in his handsome features. A light dusting of black stubble covers his square jaw, a straight nose, wide green eyes the colour of fresh grass after heavy rainfall, and a cheeky, mischievous smile that would get a girl in trouble. He's undeniably gorgeous, and with the way he's looking at me, he knows it.

Swallowing down my attraction, I tear my eyes away from his and step into the tiny office.

I drop my bag onto the small couch in the corner and look over my shoulder to find Cathal scanning me from head to toe.

"Thanks," I offer. "I owe you one."

Goosebumps erupt along my spine under his hungry gaze. "How 'bout dinner?"

"Sorry, what?" I must be hearing things. I don't know Cathal very well, but the few times we've hung out with our mutual friends, he's never shown any interest in me.

A deep rumble comes from his chest. "Dinner. You know, where you dress up, and I pick you up," he steps closer, closing the distance I put between us. "we go to a fancy restaurant, we order food, then we eat."

"Dinner? With you? As in..." I don't get to finish that sentence because Cathal steps into my personal space and lifts my chin with his strong, callous fingers. His eyes bore into mine, and I lose all ability to speak.

"A date." he finishes. "Let me take you out on a real date? I promise not to fist pump you."

Jesus, can he please stop smiling. I can't think when he does that.

Finally, I break through the lust-spell haze. "Do you ask all the ladies you save from bad dates out to dinner? What are you, some kind of Hairy Godfather? Saving all the pretty girls from catfish so that you can bed them yourself."

"I'm just going to ignore the fact that you just called me a Hairy Godfather and get straight to the point. No, I don't ask every woman I save out to dinner. Just you," he smirks.

Damn him and his lady killer dimples.

"Look, Ava, I like you. I have for a while now. Is this the best time or place to ask you out? Probably not, but I saw an opportunity, so I took it. One dinner?" he questions. "What do you say? Wanna see where this can go?"

The next words to leave my mouth both shock and excite me. "Yeah, sure. Why not?"

Cocktopus

AVA

Tonight has been the definition of strange, but at least it ended on a good note. Cathal and I arranged to meet next Friday, and I can honestly say I'm excited to see where things go.

That is until I see what, or should I say, who is asleep on my sofa.

With a loud clunk, I drop my keys into the glass bowl I keep beside the door, and Danny shoots up from his slumber like the apartment is on fire.

"Shit, Ava, you scared the crap out of me. I thought someone was breaking in."

Placing my hand against the wall, I flick off my high heeled boots while keeping my gaze lasered on my half-naked best-man-friend. "You got a fright. You're not the one who came home to find an uninvited guest drooling on her settee."

Sitting up, Danny runs his hands through his hair. "Yeah," he grumbles. "Sorry about that."

"What are you doing here? It's after midnight."

His silence is deafening, so I raise my brow — like his mother would when we were younger — and wait him out.

"I don't want to talk about it. I just need a place to crash. I was hoping I could stay with you for a few days. I need to figure some stuff out."

His deep brown eyes home in on me, sad and weary. Releasing a defeated sigh, I squeeze my eyes shut. "Yeah, of course. You can stay as long as you need."

I head towards the small kitchen, pull two beers from the fridge, twist the caps off and walk back towards my friend.

I hand him a bottle of Rockshore and gently push him for some answers. "Did something happen between you and Mandy?"

Silently, he picks at the blue and white label, acknowledging my question with the tip of his chin.

Sinking back into the couch, he flicks his head back and stares at the ceiling. "We broke up."

I know I shouldn't be happy about that statement, but '*about time*' is the first thought to cross my mind.

It's no secret that Mandy and I are anything but friends, and rightfully so. For months now, I watched from the wings as she sucked the joy out of my friend. You're probably wondering why I stood by and said nothing? The truth is it wasn't my place. Danny is big enough and bold enough to make his own life choices. As his best friend, all I can do is support him, however idiotic I think those choices may be.

"I'm sorry, Danny. I know you cared about her."

Leaning forward, he places the beer bottle on the coffee table then turns to face me. "Do you know what is worse, Avie?"

His eyes bore into mine, and for some reason, the air feels thicker. I swallow down the ginormous lump clogged in the back of my throat. "What?"

"I don't feel bad about it. Mandy and I would never have worked. We want different things. And it took me too long to figure that out."

I bite into my bottom lip and nod.

Holding back an I told you so that would rival Dolly Parton's chest, I decide to be a grown-up instead. "So, what now?"

"I don't know. That's tomorrow's problem. Tonight, I just want to hang out with my best friend and drink cheap beer."

Grabbing the remote control, I move to the free spot beside him, wrap my arms around his waist and squeeze him tight. "Done. I'll even let you pick what we're watching."

CAN SOMEONE CARE TO EXPLAIN WHY THERE'S A river of drool seeping down my chin, yet my mouth feels as though I have been chewing cotton balls?

I keep my eyes shut because I'm not quite ready to greet the morning with my middle finger. Using the cuff of my hoodie, I evict The Nile from my chin then swat at the stray hairs that came loose from my hair bobbin — those of which are inconveniently tickling my nose.

"Would you stop moving?" A deep, sexy, masculine voice muffles from beneath me. "Some of us are trying to sleep!"

Excuse me, Mr Sandman? As far as I'm aware, I'm — kind of — awake. Why am I still dreaming?

Using what little energy I have, I begin to open

my eyes, but the light beaming in my living room window forces them to shut again.

"Whoever invented the sun belongs in hell!" I grumble and shift my body weight to sit up.

Unfortunately, that doesn't happen. A large, heavy as fuck arm clamps around my waist, drawing me back and tucking me against a hard, warm chest.

Suddenly, his lips are against my ear. "Five more minutes." His warm breath brushes against my skin, sending the best kind of shivers down my spine, and I instantly relax against him.

God, it feels so good to be wrapped up like a toastie tortilla. Shimming back, the faint smell of Hugo Boss — sandalwood, vetiver, and cedar — fills my nose. It's only then I realise I'm snuggling my best friend.

My body goes rigid as my mind runs through a replay of last night.

Worst date ever.

Cathal.

I came home to find Danny asleep on the couch.

He broke up with Mandy.

One beer.

We watch Schitt's Creek's final episode and laugh our asses off at the town's new welcome sign.

Two beers.

It wouldn't be the first time I've fallen asleep on the couch with Danny. Throughout our teenage years, it was a weekly occurrence. But those innocent, adolescent sleepovers did not involve him poking me in the back with his cocktopus. *Judging by what I can feel that thing is at least eight inches.*

The sudden tingle between my thighs has my eyes shooting open. I need to move, and I need to do it now.

"Danny?" I question, keeping my voice low.

When he doesn't reply, I try again, only this time I add a little more volume.

"Danny, wake up."

"Mhmm." His reply gets dampened by my out-of-control hair. "Can't. I'm sleeping."

"Yeah, well, I gotta pee."

With far-too-much-effort-for-a-Sunday, I manage to scoot out from underneath him and roll myself over the back of the couch. My face hits the floor with an unmerciful thump, and Danny shoots up like the apartment is on fire.

His eyes scan the room until finally, he peers over the edge of the couch. "Ava?" Confusion pulls across his brow line. "What the fuck are you doing on the floor?"

I lift my head and turn my face towards him.

"Why do you ask such silly questions? Isn't it obvious? I'm dusting under the couch."

His left brow lifts when his eyes widen. "You're telling me —" he reaches for his phone off the coffee table then taps the screen "— at 6:34 on Sunday morning, you are dusting under the couch?"

I grip the back of the chair and lift myself and my dignity off the floor. When I eventually get to my feet, my left leg almost buckles from beneath me.

"AH! MY LEG! I CAN'T FEEL MY LEG!" I bounce around the room like a frog on acid, trying to get the blood circulating again.

Danny takes one look at my impromptu rendition of the cha-cha-fucking-slide and bursts into a fit of laughter.

"STOP LAUGHING, YOU SADIST! MY. LEG. IS. DEAD. DECEASED. RIP ME!" The feeling starts to return, and I squeeze my eyes shut as pins and needles travel down my calf to the tips of my toes.

Meanwhile, my best friend is in hysterics. "Did you not learn anything from the million times we watched Harry Potter?" Danny laughs. "You must not tell lies, Avie. Bad things happen when people tell lies."

If I could reach him, I'd punch him in the sperm pouch and see how he likes that, *asshole!*

"Now," he continues. "Once you stop behaving like a toddler that broke into her mother's secret chocolate stash, maybe you'll tell me why you were really face-first on the hardwood."

Diverting my gaze, I tuck my chin to my chest and mutter beneath my breath. "Yourpenistouchedme."

He cups his ear in a mocking jest, the glint in his sparkling brown eyes pisses me right off. "I'm sorry, I couldn't hear you over the noise of your embarrassment."

Ha! He thinks I'm embarrassed. Well, let's flip the roles, shall we?

I inch closer to the couch and drop down to my hunkers, so my eyes are level with his. "YOUR. PENIS. WAS. ASSAULTING. MY. ASS," I punctuate. "I was lying there, minding my business, just trying to sleep. Then I was rudely awoken by the rocket in your pocket trying to land on my full moon."

He blinks, then blinks again. Without warning, he rises from the chair and heads towards the kitchen, shouting his response over his shoulder. "It's just a bit of morning wood, Avie. I'm a man. If you slap a lump of prime beef on the table, I'm going to bite it."

"What the hell does that mean?" I ask the question that everyone's thinking. *Not that there's anyone else here. But who knows, I haven't sage'd in a while, so there could be some ghost floating about.*

He turns abruptly, and I almost plough into him. "It means we fell asleep. You were wiggling your ass, and my cock approved."

He pulls open the cabinets then slams them shut, searching for — what I presume is — something to eat. When he is unsuccessful, he turns, leans against the counter, and folds his glorious arms across his chiselled chest. "Sorry if it weirded you out. It won't happen again."

It takes everything in me to hide my what-if-I-want-it-to reaction, but somehow, I manage to plaster on a smile. "Don't worry! I'll forgive you. Let's just forget about it."

He nods, then holds out his hand for me to shake. "Deal?"

Reaching forward, I take his hand and say, "Deal!"

"Now that's settled," he prompts. "I need food. My belly hurts."

The fact that he called it a belly is laughable. The

man's ripped. I'm pretty sure there'd be more fat on a butchers pencil.

"You promised me breakfast, remember?"

Recognition dawns on his face. "That's right. I did."

"The Rusty Spoon?" I bat my lashes and smile wide.

He rolls his eyes at my excitement. "Do we ever eat anywhere else?"

"No! But that's because your brother owns the place, and he gives me extra bacon with my French toast."

Extra Bacon

DANNY

I won't pretend Ava's reaction this morning didn't bum me out because it did.

When I first realised, she was in my arms, I thought I was dreaming. I hate to admit; I loved having her pressed against my chest as her sweet, sugary, candy-floss scent surrounded me.

It stirred up something. Something that, until recently, I didn't know I was missing.

Then, she bound off the couch as if her knickers had gone up in flames. She seemed genuinely shook about us spooning, and I had no idea what to do with that. So, instead, I made up some half-assed excuse as to why my dick was standing at attention, and thankfully, she bought it.

"Are you doing okay over there?" Ava interrupts my thoughts. "You're awfully quiet."

"Yeah, sorry. I'm away with the fairies."

For the first time since we arrived at The Rusty Spoon, I allow myself to *really* look at her. She has piled her pale pink hair on top of her head — in two separate buns — but her Smurf-blue fringe hangs down over her black-framed glasses, hiding the brightness of her ocean blue eyes. Although her face is almost free from make-up, she is wearing a bold pink colour on her lips.

Quirky, slightly awkward, but gorgeous, nonetheless.

"What are you looking at?" She lifts her hand and pats her cheek. "Do I have something on my face?"

Thankfully, before I can reply with something I shouldn't — like no, you're just gorgeous, and I think I might be in love with you — my brother Keegan walks over and hands us our usual order. Full Irish breakfast for me, and French toast with bacon and maple syrup, for Ava.

"Good morning, Ava." He plasters on one of his playboy grins. "Looking flawless as always." He places the plates on the table and nods towards Ava's plate. "I gave you some extra bacon."

The smile she gives him makes my chest tight. Jesus, I need to control myself. This new-found jealousy is driving me insane. Keegan is my brother, and he is well aware of my ridiculous crush on my eccentric yet stunning best friend.

"Why thank you, you don't look so bad yourself, Keegan," she winks.

My brother's eyes briefly flick to mine, and I send him a warning glare. *She is off-limits!*

Chuckling to himself, he turns back to Ava. "So, how was your date?" He wiggles his brow.

I forgot about her date. After everything with Mandy, it must have slipped my mind.

"It was an epic fail. Not only did Barry look nothing like his profile picture, but he also spent the entire meal fist pumping me like a loony bin."

"You're joking."

"Oh, Keegan!" Ava quips. "I wish I were. I was so mortified."

The horrified look on her face is comical. She dives into a rundown of the night, and Keegan and I can't stop laughing.

"The night wasn't a total write off," she adds.

"Yeah?" Keegan questions. "Why is that?"

A shy smile creeps across her face, and a hint of blush appears on her cheeks.

Keegan's eyes dart in my direction, and he smirks at me. "Did you two —"

"No! God, no! Never!" Ava states with a nervous laugh. I sip my coffee and swallow down the feeling her words bring.

"Cathal asked me out."

WHAT. THE. FUCK! The mouthful of coffee sprays from my lips as I break into a coughing fit.

Keegan's hand slams down on my back. "You okay?"

I level him with an I-will-knock-you-out glare, and he laughs harder. *Bollox!*

"Sorry," I say once I've caught my breath. "Wrong pipe."

"I'm sure that was it," Keegan mutters before adding, "Right you two, I gotta get back to the kitchen. Enjoy."

Once my brother is safely out of earshot, I turn to Avie. "So, Cathal Daly? How did that come about?"

"Erm, he saved me from my date, then asked me out."

She stuffs a fork full of food into her mouth. "He's hot, so I said yes."

Cathal Daly is a member at my da's gym and has

been since we were teens, and although we don't run in the same circles, we've hung out a few times with mutual friends. He seems like a nice bloke, but he has a long list of women who have occupied his bed. There are so many objections ringing between my ears. But I know no matter what excuse I give, Ava won't listen. She's got a stubborn side, and if she wants to do something, nobody, not even me, can stop her.

But fuck'd if I'll allow Ava to become another notch on his post.

She deserves better. I am aware I sound like a jealous prick. The problem is, I don't know how to fix it. The feelings I have for Ava are not new, but they are growing stronger by the day. I need to get a grip of myself before I shoot my mouth and say something, something I'll most likely regret. I need my head and my heart on the same page, pronto.

My brothers and I have always reserved Sunday afternoons for Maura O'Donoghue, and as much as us boys bitch and moan about family time, we wouldn't have it any other way. My mouth waters as the sweet smell of lamb roasting wafts from my mother's kitchen.

"Ma, are you sure you don't want any help?" Keegan shouts from his spot on the couch. Every week he asks her the same question, and every time she gives him the same reply.

"No, you stay where you are, sweetheart. You've been cooking for the entire town all week."

"When are you going to learn, Son?" Dad laughs. "You may be the best chef this town has, but everything you know, you learned in your mammy's kitchen."

"He went to the best culinary school in Ireland," Kye snorts. "Pretty sure he knows more than what his mamma taught him."

"Kye!" My ma's voice travels through the open archway, scolding my brother with her tone alone.

"Sorry, Ma!"

"So," Keegan seeks me out. "What's the story with you, D?

How're things with Mandy?"

"Are you still sleeping on the couch?" Kye adds, making Keegan laugh.

"For your information, I am still sleeping on a couch, just not Mandy's." Silence falls over the room. "We broke up."

A loud thud of banging pots booms from the kitchen, followed quickly by the pitter-patter of my mother's feet.

Suddenly, Maura O'Donoghue rushes into the living room with a wooden spoon in hand. "Thank God above. I've been praying for this day for the past eight months. I lit a candle every Sunday after Mass, and finally, the Lord answered my prayers."

Okay, Ma! A little dramatic, don't you think?

Her tiny hands grip my face and squeeze my cheeks. "That girl was not for you, son. She would have drained you dry and then slept with your brother out of spite."

"Excuse you." My brothers shout simultaneously, both horrified at her accusation.

She looks over her shoulder. "Whist you two! You know what I mean. The woman was a sponge."

I'm a little shocked at my mother's dislike. In all the times I brought Mandy over for Sunday dinner — which was not that often — my mother never expressed her disapproval to me. I thought she was pleased that I was finally settling down and hoping that I would give her grandbabies. How wrong was I?

"Where are you staying?" She stands, straightening her apron. "Do you need me to make up the bed in your old room?"

As much as I love my mother, moving back home at twenty-nine is a giant NO-NO! Maura is not known for giving people space, and frankly, I don't enjoy her hovering over me. Besides, she is like the news of the world, always gossiping. If you want the entire town to know what you're up to, tell-a-gram, tell-a-phone, tell-my-mother.

"Nah! I'm good. Avie said I could crash at hers for as long as I need."

A fond smile graces my mother's lips. "She's a good girl. Why can't you pluck up the courage I rared you to have and ask her out? She'd make a lovely daughter-in-law. Wouldn't she, Peter?"

My eyes roll as my Da grunts out a reply, his eyes never wavering from the GAA match on the television. For years, it's been the same thing. Anytime I am single, my mother insists I ask Ava out. And every time, I answer her with the same reply, "We're just ___"

"Friends!" They all shout in unison, cutting me off.

It's official. I need a new family.

Everything Is On Fire

AVA

"Honey, I'm home." I peel off my cherry red Doc Marten boots and place them in the shoe rack beside the hall door.

It's been almost a week since Danny came to stay with me, and I have to admit, I love having him here. He's cleaner than Kim and Aggie from that show, *How Clean is Your House*. He cooks every evening, and even though he wakes up at the butt crack of dawn to get to the gym early, he makes me fresh coffee before he goes, so I'll forgive him. To be honest, at the rate he is going, I won't let him leave.

Making my way up my tiny hallway, I follow the delicious smell wafting from my kitchen.

I poke my head through the open doorway and nearly swallow my tongue.

Illegal! No man should be allowed to look that good while wearing nothing but grey tracksuit bottoms and a 'Straight Outta the 90's' apron. I repeat, no man.

Jesus, why aren't the smoke alarms going off? Cause let me tell you, everything is on fire! And by everything, I mean me.

His slightly long, brown hair is tied back into a small bun, showcasing his sharp jawline and high-lighting his defined cheekbones. A light dusting of stubble graces his face, and all I want to do is sit on it.

Hold your horses, Horney Helen! Nobody will be sitting on anything.

My eyes travel over the exposed, defined muscles of his back, and suddenly I have the urge to run my tongue over every tattoo. Every. Single. One.

"Hey, you're home early. How was work?"

I shake away the dirty video montage that seems to be on repeat in my mind and remind myself that we can never go there. Ever!

Stepping into the alcove kitchen, I squeeze by Danny and lean against the counter. "Yeah, my last client never showed, so I got to duck out a little early. What are you making? It smells awesome."

Angling his head slightly, he flashes me a smile that would disintegrate the knickers off a nun. Pair that with the depths of his brown eyes, and I'm stunned, speechless.

Some women love arms and shoulders. For me, it's all about the smile — the kind that reaches the eyes and makes the entire world halt. Unfortunately for me, that's precisely why I'm falling for my best friend.

"Garlic butter potatoes, roasted carrot and parsnip with honey glazed onions, and T-bone steak."

All my favourites.

My stomach grumbles out in approval, and Danny's shoulders shake. "I take it you're hungry."

"Starving." *In more ways than one.* But I keep that piece of information to myself.

"Do I have time for a quick shower?"

Wiping his hands, he drapes the tea-towel over his shoulder. "Yeah, you should be good. Dinner will be ready in about fifteen minutes."

"Cool." I shimmy past him, taking extra care not to brush against him. "Thanks for cooking. You don't have to cook every night, though? I can make dinner for us, too."

His eyebrow lifts.

"Stop looking at me like that! My cooking is not that bad."

Without thinking, I reach out to slap his chest, but his hand grips my wrist before I can make contact. The skin beneath his touch scorches, and I take a step back, which was an awful idea — since my kitchen is the size of a cardboard shoebox. Something hits the back of my calf, and suddenly I'm stumbling backwards over the recycle bin. Like lightning, Danny's arm skates around my waist, stopping me from colliding with the partition wall that separates the kitchen and living space. He tugs me forward, and I land face-first into his chest.

"Are you okay?"

I tilt my face and peek up at him over my lashes. "Um-hmm."

The space between us is minimal, and the urge to kiss him takes over my brain cells.

His woodsy scent immobilises me, stealing every molecule of air from my lungs. I breathe in, but that only makes my unexpected need worsen.

Danny lifts his hand, carefully sweeping the stray hairs from my eyes. "Ava?"

I'm lost in the moment, savouring his gentle caress when the smoke alarm begins to wail.

"Shit." Danny snaps out of whatever come-fuckery was happening between us. He drops his arm from my waist and turns to attend to the smoking frying pan.

"I'm just gonna," I point toward the bathroom. "Erm, yeah."

"Avie, wait."

I pretend not to hear him, which we both know is virtually impossible since my apartment is smaller than a new-born baby's belly button.

IT'S NO SECRET. I AM THE MOST AWKWARD PERSON I've ever met. I don't do well under certain circumstances, constantly stumbling over my words or even myself. Some of the things to leave my mouth ought to be illegal, but there's always been one person on the planet that doesn't seem to mind my obscene level of nuthouse crazy — Danny.

After that near encounter in the kitchen, I couldn't bear to look at him, so I locked myself in the bathroom. Now, here I am, hiding in the confines of my shower, daydreaming about Danny's rough hands roaming over my love button, desperately wanting him to push it, push it real good.

God, what is wrong with me? We have been friends all our lives, and now all of a sudden, I am a polar bear stranded in the desert — out of my fucking depth.

The need I feel between my thighs is unbearable. My vajayjay hasn't had a good service in almost a year, and I'm aching for a good oil change. But I'd be loony to think Danny is the right mechanic for the job. Sure, he has abs that would grate cheese; and judging by what I've seen of his cock-monster, he would hit all the right spots.

But no, we can't cross that line, no matter how much I, or my tunnel of love, want to.

I could never risk our friendship like that; it's far too important to me.

I need to move forward and stop fantasising about my best friend fucking me on the kitchen counter. From now on, I am placing Danny back in the friends-only, can't-touch-this zone.

Pursuing something would only end in tears, and I am the world's ugliest crier — nobody wants to witness that. Besides, he practically lives here now, and if I were to cross a line, and my feelings are not reciprocated, I would have to go into hiding. They don't have bacon in hiding, so that's not an option either.

Realising I can't hide away forever, I step out of the shower, dry off, and quickly pull on my loungewear. I run the brush through my long unicorn coloured hair and sigh. I need to top up my colour. Maybe Charlie can squeeze me in for a touch-up tomorrow between clients because everyone knows roots are for trees, not people.

Leaving the bathroom, I decide that tomorrow, I will go out on my first date with Cathal, and if all goes to plan, I can move on from this ridiculous crush.

TO SAY DINNER IS UNCOMFORTABLE WOULD BE A VAST understatement. Danny and I have barely spoken two words to each other, and the lack of communication between us is starting to get on my nerves. I pop another potato into my mouth and groan a little louder than socially acceptable. "God! This is so good."

A cheeky smile curls at the corner of Danny's lips, highlighting the slight wink he threw my way. "Glad you're enjoying it."

Aha! There he is.

"So, how's work?"

"It's okay, I guess. I've spoken to Charlie, and we're thinking of opening our own place soon. It's only in the planning stages, but hopefully, we can get the money together. We have enough regular clients built up that they'd come with us."

I ramble on some more, but Danny never loses interest. He's hung up on every word I say.

Finally, when I finish my PowerPoint presentation, he chimes in. "That's awesome, Avie. If you need anything, just let me know. I'll do whatever I can to help you reach your dreams."

It's moments like this one where I realise how lucky I am to have him in my life. One day, he's going to make some lucky bitch very happy, such a shame it won't be me.

Pushing back my disappointment, I ask, "What about you? How's the training going?"

He has been preparing for his next fight for weeks now, and although it's still a few months away, he has to be on top of his game. It's the fight he's been waiting for, the one that will either make or break his career.

Danny's dad, Peter, runs Game On Fitness — the leading mixed martial arts academy in Ireland. Over the years, the gym has produced several Ultimate Fighting Champions, and I have zero doubt that

Danny will be the next name added to the awe-inspiring list.

"It's going well. I still have a lot of work to do, but I'm confident."

"And so you should be," I point to his arms. "Just look at those guns."

Just like that, we are back to normal. Awky-mo-mo, forgotten.

The Moms On Tiktok

AVA

"I'D RIDE YOU," I TELL MYSELF AS I STARE AT MY reflection in my bedroom mirror. Thankfully, Charlie touched-up my roots and squeezed me in for a curly blow-dry, so my hair took little to no effort on my part. My cropped, floral-print top showcases my girls' curves to perfection, making my less-than-stellar chest look pretty-f-ing-perfect. I've paired my favourite high waisted, black, faux leather leggings with my holographic stilettos to finish off my outfit, making me look both sweet and sexy.

I kept my make-up simple, adding a thin layer of

foundation, a bold pink lip, and a 50's style wing liner. I twirl around, look over my shoulder, and check out my ass. "Yes! That right there is the reason I squat like Chris Hemsworth is behind me."

Lifting my iPhone off the vanity, I click the small button on the side, and the screen lights up.

Shit! I'm meeting Cathal in fifteen minutes.

My stomach flips as my nerves take over. I'm unsure about tonight, but after that near kiss with Danny last night, I know I need to power through my reservations and see this date through.

I pucker my lips one last time, then flash my best Chandler Bing impression at the mirror, double-checking my lipstick is not coating my teeth. Once I deem myself first-date ready, I grab my phone and clutch and head down the hall.

Just as I pick my keys off the hallstand, the front door opens, and in walks, my sweat covered best friend/new roomie. Deep brown eyes that remind me of melted Belgian chocolate roam over every inch of my body, making me feel very conscious about my outfit choice.

"What are you doing here? I thought you were at the gym late tonight?"

Danny's eyes finally find mine, and I suck in a needed breath. His lips curl to the left, giving me his signature half-smile. "I hurt my knee, so dad sent me home to rest up. Doesn't want me to overdo it."

"OH SHIT! Are you okay?"

He drops his bag to the floor with a chuckle. "I'm grand. Don't worry. Dad's only taking precautions. I just need to rest for a day or two."

"Are you sure? I can call Cathal and cancel."

He's silent for a beat as if he's contemplating my offer, but then his brows furrow. "No. Go, enjoy your night. I'm just going to have a hot shower and chill out."

I can't help but feel bad. If our roles reversed, I know that Danny would drop everything to look after me without a doubt. Before I can protest, he grips my shoulders with his callous hands. "Stop overthinking it, Avie. I'll be fine."

My shoulder's sag as I blow out a breath. "Fine. But if you need anything at all, call me, okay?"

"Anything?" He quips with a raised brow.

I slap his chest. "Get your head out of the gutter."

Leaning forward, he brushes his lips against my forehead.

"Go! Get out of here before I change my mind." My eyes shoot wide as my limbs go rigid. Danny kissed me! Okay, so maybe I'm a tad dramatic. It was a peck on the head at best. But regardless of where, his lips were still on me, and if I'm honest with myself, I want them on me again. Preferably somewhere in the nether region.

Fortunately, he retreats down the tiny hallway before I can voice my thoughts.

Thank fuck for that!

I'VE LOST MY MIND!

I'm sitting in a fancy as fuck restaurant, eating food I can't even pronounce, and drinking wine that costs more than I earn in a day at my nine-to-five job at BedHeads.

Across from me sits one of the sexiest men this town has to offer, and get this, he's wearing a crisp white shirt that's rolled up to his elbows, exposing noteworthy forearms I want to lick. He's got that signature romance-book-boyfriend-look. You know the ones — dark hair, green eyes, and chiselled bone structure that would make the moms on TikTok weep. Cathal Daly is the kind of man that vibrators are made for — not as a replacement, but to envision while you ride the wave all the way to orgasm city.

And yet, I feel nothing.

Okay, so there may be a tiny tingle because hello, I'm not blind.

This man could sit proudly on a cover in The New York Times bestseller list, providing all the horney women of the world a taste of the untouchable — but I'm not feeling it. And for the life of me, I don't know why?

He's funny, charming, and extremely attentive. Did I mention sex-on-a-stick gorgeous? But like the idiot I am, my mind is stuck on the unattainable — my best friend.

Ugh, I'm so mad at Danny. How dare he ruin my date when he's not even in the building!

"You're not feeling this, are you?" Cathal breaks through my thoughts.

I release a sigh and lift my wine glass to my lips. Before I take a sip, I reply, "I'm sorry. Is it that obvious?"

He scoffs back a deep laugh. "Nah! But you look exactly how I feel."

Exsqueeze-me. Did he just say he's not feeling my company? Rude!

Shocked by his blatant displeasure, I choke on my wine.

"Shit!" He retracts. "I didn't mean that how it

sounded. You just look like you are hoping I was someone else."

"Does that mean you wish I were someone else?"

Shamelessly, he nods his reply.

I should be offended, but that would be a little pot calling the kettle. So, instead, I make the most of my free meal and offer Cathal some womanly advice.

"Okay, correct me if I'm wrong here... Let's say there is this girl. We'll call her Danielle. You have some feelings for her but telling her would ruin a life-long friendship. So, instead, you asked out the prettiest girl you could find, all so you could try to move forward from the crush you are harbouring for her. But halfway through the meal with this girl, who by the way is hotter than Satan's ass crack, you realise it doesn't matter how utterly fuckable this chick is — you're so hung-up on Danielle that it will never work."

Cathal sits back with wide eyes, resting his shoulders against the leather booth. Tilting the neck of his beer bottle, he points it toward me. "You're good."

"Why thank you!"

"So, how did you guess all that? Are you a secret psychic or something?"

"Nah!" I shrug my shoulder. "I'm just deflecting my shit on you."

"Even so, I shouldn't have asked you out when I'm hung up on someone else. I'm sorry."

I see it in his eyes, the same tug-o-war I'm wrestling with all week.

"Don't worry about it. I haven't exactly been the best company either, and if you wanna play the blame game, I shouldn't have accepted."

He's quiet for a moment, then suddenly, he leans forward, resting his elbows on the table.

"For what it's worth, I had a great time, Ava. You're a great girl. Gorgeous, funny, and you don't pull any punches. I hope whoever it is you're pining after recognises how great you are."

Flattered by his swoon-worthy response, I reply, "Thanks, but I'll be okay. One day, hopefully soon, I will stop pining over the one man I can't have, and I'll live happily ever after, preferably with a dog, because cats freak me out."

Raising his glass in a toast, Cathal shouts, "To the ones we can't have."

I smile and join in. "May they forever wonder what they're missing."

After our revelation, things between Cathal and I shifted from a date to a regular night-out-with-a-friend.

Deciding there was no point in wasting the

evening, we headed to the nearest bar and ended up having a great night. I never mentioned Danny, and Cathal never did tell me who he was pining for, although I have a sneaky suspicion, it has something to do with his best friend's girl.

The night comes to an end, and Cathal, being the gentleman he is, walks me home. We get to my front door, and he pulls me into a friendly hug.

"Thanks for a great night, Ava. That was the most fun I've had in a long time."

He steps back, releasing me from his hold. "We should do it again, sometime."

"As friends," I add with a drunken giggle.

"As friends."

Walking backwards, Cathal retreats down the hallway.

"Cathal?" I call out, stopping him in his tracks. "For what it's worth, Charlie would be lucky to have you. You're a great guy."

His eyes go wide with surprise. "How did you—"

"I'm a secret psychic, remember. And don't worry, your secret is safe with me."

He releases a breath, and his shoulders visibly drop with relief. "Thanks, appreciate it."

"No problem. Word of advice, though, you

should tell her. You never know. She may feel the same."

His lips lift into a smile. "Tell you what, I'll think about it. But only if you think about telling Danny, too."

"How did —" I chuckle. "Nevermind."

"Goodnight, Avie."

"Night."

Roller Skates, Unicorns, Doughnuts, And Me

DANNY

IT'S FOUR AM, MY KNEE IS THROBBING, AND FOR THE life of me, I can't get comfy on this piece-of-shit sofa bed. As I shift onto my side, I rearrange the pillow beneath my head.

A pain like I've never felt darts through my kneecap. My jaw tightens, and I grind my teeth. Closing my eyes, I try — and fail — to push through the agony. "FUCK!"

I pull forward, and using my palms, I sit up straight, then scoot back against the back of the couch.

Suddenly the overhead light flickers on, illuminating the living room. Ava rushes toward me in nothing but a t-shirt, her hair piled like a bird's nest on the top of her head.

"Are you okay? I heard you screaming like a banshee from the bedroom," she scrambles, sinking down onto the edge of the sofa bed.

"I was not screaming!"

Her lips pull into her signature are-you-shitting-me pout as she calls me out with her rounded blues. "I beg to differ."

I take in her dishevelment. There are black smudges under her eyes that remind me of a panda, smeared lipstick stains her cheeks, and I'm pretty sure that's dried drool on her chin, but even though she looks as though someone has dragged her through a hedge kicking and screaming, never have I wanted to kiss her more.

I blink away that thought and apologise, "Sorry for waking you. My knee is killing me, and this couch is not helping matters."

Something flickers in her eyes, and when she opens her mouth, I realise it's guilt. "Oh, my God, I'm a terrible friend. I should have offered you the bed. I was too busy rushing out to meet Cathal, and it never dawned on me."

Ignoring the jealousy boiling beneath the surface, I grunt, "I'm not going to steal your bed, Avie. I'll be fine."

Determined to prove her wrong, I swing my legs over the side, plant my feet on the floor and hike myself up.

Oh, my fucking shit, I shouldn't have done that!

Shifting my weight onto my right leg, I move toward the kitchen, ignoring Ava and her curious gaze.

"You're limping," she follows me, pointing out the obvious.

"You're hovering." I search through her cabinets, looking for anything to dull the excruciating throb. "Have you any Diafine?" I twist my head, looking over my shoulder.

She pulls out a pint glass, fills it with some cold water, and passes it to me without a word.

I take a sip, watching as she climbs up onto the countertop, shimming her way over to the overhead press above the refrigerator.

"What in God's name are you doing?"

She turns, glaring at me. "I'm getting you some pain killers."

"I could have got them. You didn't need to put on a professional parkour show."

She hops down with ease and shoves the packet of anti-inflammatories at my chest. "Excuse you! We're not all descendants of bigfoot. I've learned to embrace my less-than-miniature height. If you think that was bad, you should watch me climb into the attic to get my Christmas decorations. It's an Olympic sport."

"Now," she continues, "take those, and let's get back to bed. My head is throbbing from my self-inflicted alcohol consumption."

I swallow down the two pills underneath her watchful eye. Wrapping my left arm around her waist, I pull her in close, place a quick, fleeting kiss on her forehead, and step back. "Thanks for the meds. Night."

"Oh no, you don't!" Ava grips my elbow. "You are not sleeping on that couch for another second. You can sleep with me tonight."

There's a sentence I never thought I'd hear her say. Not that she means it the way I hoped, but a man can dream.

"Are you sure?"

"Yes, yes, I'm sure. You're in pain, and you need a proper bed. Just keep to your side, and for the love of your balls, don't hog the blankets. I'll clean out the spare bedroom tomorrow, and hopefully, we can source you a proper bed."

"Ava, you don't have to do that. This was only meant to be temporary. I don't want you giving up your in-home salon because I need a place to crash."

"You're my best friend. If our roles were reversed, you would have given me your bed. Besides, what if you moved in here permanently? I like having you around, and I wouldn't say no to the extra help with paying my mortgage."

The rest of my life flashes before my eyes, me and her, the house, us cuddling on the couch after a long day at work, and X-rated porn-worthy sex sessions that last hours on end once we put the kids to bed. It's then I realise, no matter how hard I try to get over the feelings I have for my best friend, nobody will ever live up to the idea of her in my head.

She's it for me, always has been. Now, I just need to find a way to prove that to her without ruining everything we've spent our lives building.

"If you're sure?"

Rolling her eyes, Ava shakes her head. "D, I love you, but if you don't stop overthinking this, I will murder you while you're sleeping. I'm tired, tethering somewhere between maybe-still-a-little-drunk and possibly-just-hungover. I'm heading to bed. I need to sleep off the fog settling behind my eyes. If you want it, the right side is yours, so make up your mind before you have an aneurysm."

AVA

The morning sun peaks through the small gap in my curtains, reminding me that drinking my body weight in Sambuca was probably not the best idea I've ever had. I squeeze my eyes tight, not ready to face the evil glare of the sun.

Why do I do this to myself?

When I was twenty-one, I could down shots like no tomorrow. But now, the death of my youth is quickly approaching, and I can't keep up.

I wrap myself up in my duvet as waves of nausea add to my stream of misery.

The bed shifts beneath me, and I freeze. My lungs tighten, trapping any air inside. I take a mental scan of my physical body and thank Jehovah's Witnesses, I'm wearing my Central Perk sleep shirt, and my unicorn's don't fart knickers. *There is no way I had a one-night stand if I'm wearing these knickers. Talk about killing the mood!*

Slowly, I turn my head, peeking over my shoulder

at the person in question, and my lungs expand with a relieved sigh.

Thank God, for a moment there, I thought I'd done something stupid like sleep with a stranger while highly intoxicated.

Been there, done that, and have zero desire to do it again.

Suddenly, last night rushes to the forefront of my mind, and I roll over onto my side and face Danny. My unicorn duvet is wrapped around him, making me snort. He looks adorable with his so-beautiful-it-hurts-to-look-at-him body, curled up in sparkles and glitter. His thick, dark brows are relaxed, and his long, black lashes kiss his cheekbones. My fingers itch, begging me to reach out and brush the fly-away strands from his face.

After my date with Cathal, I realised I am so bad at love because my heart already belongs to someone. Things with Danny could be fantastic. He knows me better than anyone in the world, and he fully accepts me for who I am — a loud-mouthed, sarcastic weirdo who is more awkward than someone who wears Nike and still can't do it.

I need to talk to him, and soon. The problem is I don't know how to broach the subject. It's not exactly something you announce over a bag of fish and chips. Can you imagine the horror? *Oh, hey, so I know we've been friends since our womb raider days, but somewhere between preschool and puberty, I kinda, sorta, maybe, fell in love with you* — no, thank you! I'd rather sit on Sonic.

I'll have to come up with another way, like drop some subtle hints. Yes! I can do that.

Turning slightly, I blindly reach over to my bedside locker and feel around for my phone.

My arm flails, swatting the wooden top. "Where are you, you international spying device? I could have sworn I plugged you in last night," I mutter, trying to remain quiet, so I don't wake Danny up.

Somehow, I end up bent like a pretzel, my arm at an unnatural angle. It would be some much easier to roll over, but I'm enjoying the view. Finally, after far too much energy, I find it. "Gotcha!"

The screen lights up, assaulting my pupils and highlighting the WhatsApp message from Charlie.

Charlie: Hey, how was your date with Mr forearms?

A laugh rumbles up my chest, squeezing by my lips at the arm-flex and lick emojis.

Turning down the volume on my phone, I silence the clicking sound the buttons make when I type and text her back.

**Ava: I woke up with a man in my bed...
spoiler alert: it wasn't my date.**

The three dots jump across my screen, and I
know she is hyperventilating like an English teacher
explaining essay writing — she needs to know all the
basics, the who, what, when, where, and why's?

**Charlie: Oh, I have so many questions.
Who is it? Do we know him? What size is
his penis? Details, Ava. I NEED DETAILS!**

Opening my camera app, I point my phone at
Danny, turn off the flash, snap a picture and forward
it to Charlie.

**Charlie: OH MY FUCKIN' SHIT!!! Please tell
me you finally jumped on his pogo stick?**

She texts back immediately, and I laugh a little
too loud, waking the sleeping Adonis beside me.
Danny stirs, and I hold my breath as his eyes blink
open. His tongue pokes out, running along his
bottom lip, and my nostrils flare. His smile is slow and
lazy, but it stirs a pool of desire in my gut.

"Good morning." His sleepy eyes hold my gaze,

and the heart in my chest bounces around like Zac Efron in High School Musical 2.

"What's so funny?"

"What?"

"You were laughing." He raises his hands to his face, rubbing the sleep from his eyes.

My eyes flick to my iPhone screen, and I quickly lock it so he can't see my text thread. "Oh, nothing. Just Charlie being Charlie."

I place my phone on the locker and turn back to face him. "So, how did you sleep? You looked very cosy, wrapped up in my unicorns.

He looks down, his eyes landing on the large image of a unicorn roller skating while eating a doughnut, and he laughs.

"I was so tired; I didn't notice how ridiculous these sheets are."

I grab my chest, mocking shock at his statement. "How dare you say my sheets are ridiculous. They're awesome. All my favourite things in one place. Roller skates, unicorns, and doughnuts, what's not to like?"

"And me!"

"Sorry, what?"

"All your favourite things in one place — roller skates, unicorns, doughnuts, and me."

I swat at his bare chest. "You wish, big man. You wish."

He mutters something under his breath, but I don't quite catch it.

I'm nearly sure it was *'Yeah, I do',* but that can't be right, can it?

Clean Up On Aisle V

AVA

"So," Danny prompts while stirring the scrambled eggs with a wooden spoon, stopping them from sticking to the frying pan. "Have you decided on what you want to do for your birthday next week?"

I roll my eyes. I don't particularly appreciate talking about the upcoming celebration of my day of birth. I'm turning thirty, and I don't know about others, but it's not exactly something I want to celebrate. It serves as a reminder of all the shit I've yet to accomplish.

I had all these hopes growing up, and I always

thought by the ripe old age of thirty, I would have my shit together, but the reality is, I don't even know where my shit is.

I'm nowhere near where I hoped I'd be at this age. I don't own my own business. I don't have a husband to hold me at night, and no children are running around, destroying my house but filling my heart with love.

Sure, I own my own home — if you could even call it that — it's not exactly the Ritz, but it's mine. Do I love the fact that it's so tiny I couldn't swing a cat in it? No, but you know what they say, beggars can't be choosers.

"I told you, I don't want to do anything. I plan on staying at home all day, wearing all black while I listen to my 90's playlist on repeat, mourning the good ole days."

Danny laughs. "Ava! How many times do I have to tell you, you can't hold a funeral for your twenties?"

Pushing off the counter, I saunter to the fridge and pull out the orange juice. "Yes, I can. They deserve a proper send-off. They were the best days of my life. Pretty soon, I will be riddled with arthritis, only eating food that's hea... I can't even say it."

Danny plates our breakfast and carries them

towards the living room. "I think the word you're looking for is healthy."

Following him, I scoff. "Please refrain from using that word in my house. You'll offend my doughnuts, bread-rolls, and cream."

Together we take a seat on the couch, and Danny passes me my plate. "You're one of a kind, Ava Marie McCann."

"Right back at you, Daniel Peter O'Donoghue."

I pick up the remote and turn on my television, scrolling until I find my Netflix app. Clicking the recently watched section, I press play on Suits.

We eat in silence as Mike tries to save some single mother from losing their apartment to greedy developers.

Finally, like a fat penguin, Danny breaks the ice. "Did you mean what you said last night?"

Fear grapples up my throat. What the hell did I say? Did I throw myself at him, or worse, feel him up as he lay beside me?

Deciding to play dumber than a cast member of Geordie Shore, I question, "What exactly did I say last night?"

"You don't remember?"

"Erm... no, not exactly."

Danny gently places his now empty plate on the

coffee table and turns to face me. A pensive look darkens his eyes. "You offered to clear out your home salon so I could move in... more permanently."

Did I? Well, I suppose that would be the logical thing to do. It's not like he can continue to sleep on my tiny couch. The man is well over six-foot.

I shovel the last spoonful of deliciously fluffy scrambled egg into my mouth, and my taste buds scream out their approval. Would having Danny here full-time be such a bad thing?

No, no, it wouldn't. But it means I can't tell him how I feel about him, at least not anytime soon. That would make our living arrangement far from ideal, especially if my feelings are not reciprocated.

He's my friend, and he needs a place to stay, sure he could probably move back in with his parents, but moving in here would make the most sense, mainly since he spends his free time here anyway.

"Oh, yeah, that," I pretend. "of course, I meant it. We can clear out the room today if it suits your schedule?"

"Only if you're sure. I don't want to impose."

"You won't be. I like having someone here. I toyed around with the idea of a pet for company, and you're like a dog, only you clean up after yourself. So, it's a win-win for me."

"I'm going to ignore the fact you compared me to a four-legged creature and head straight to thank you."

"You're welcome. Now, text your mother and let her know you won't be around for Sunday dinner. That spare room won't empty itself."

"WHAT THE FUCK ARE IN THESE BOXES? THEY WEIGH a tonne."

"Aren't you some big MMA fighter? Why are you complaining? You work out seventeen hours a day, six days a week."

"It's eight hours, but that's beside the point."

Danny flips open the flap of the box he took from the back of the wardrobe in what will be his new room.

"Photographs! I'm breaking my back for photographs."

Plonking my ass on the light grey carpet beside him, I peer into the box and burst out laughing. I reach in, pulling out the 4x6 picture.

"Do you remember this?" I question, shoving the image in his face.

Danny focuses on the captured memory and

smiles wide.

"That was the year we decided to swap Halloween costumes for Charlie's Halloween party."

"Not gonna lie, you look fucking ridiculous," I laugh harder, the tears gathering in my lash line.

"Of course, I do! I'm wearing a school shirt tied above my belly button, a school skirt, and knee-high socks."

"I thought you made a great Britney Spears," I snort.

"Of course you did. You weren't the one with the wind tickling your testicles."

"No, I had it way worse."

"What makes you think that?" He quips, laughter dancing around his eyes.

"I'm wearing a genie costume, and the spout of the lamp is right at my crotch. Do you have any idea how many people tried to rub me that night?"

"Ha. Ha. Ha."

Danny sets the photo down and pulls out another. This one is a little older than the last.

"Oh, this was your eighth birthday," he announces like he remembers the day as if it was yesterday. "You were super pissed because Suzie broke your Spice Girl piñata."

Danny picked up all the broken pieces and glued

them back together with Pritt-stick so I could have another turn at busting it open.

Looking down at the photo, I recall the exact moment it was taken—the moment Danny handed me the newly glued Spice Up Your Life piñata. The smile on my face is so broad it's touching my eyes.

That was the day I fell, entirely and utter in love with my best friend.

I lean over, resting my head against his shoulder. "You were an awesome friend."

His head rests on mine. "Were?"

"Are!" I correct. "You are an awesome friend."

We spend the next hour or so looking back at a lifetime of shared moments, everyone more precious than the last. We've shared so much — first days of school, first school dances, first family holidays. He's been there for it all.

For a moment, I allow myself to picture sharing the rest of my life with him too.

The images flash before my eyes with ease, frightening the ever-loving shit out of me — our first pet, our wedding day, our forever home, and our first child, each one forcing butterflies to take flight in my stomach.

"Danny?"

His lips brush against my crazy hair. "Yeah, Avie."

"Can you promise me something?"

"Anything," he replies without hesitation.

"Promise me that no matter where our lives take us, you'll always be my best friend."

His arm circles my waist, and he pulls me tighter against his chest. "Don't worry, babe. I'm not going anywhere."

Ignoring the fact that he called me babe, I nestle a little closer. "Me neither."

The rest of the afternoon passes by in a blur of boxes. And before I know it, we have the room emptied, and my stomach is crying out for attention. I flop backwards and stare at the ceiling. "I'm exhausted. Who knew I could be such a hoarder?"

"I did," Danny announces. "You've got every moment of your life tucked away in boxes."

"I do not!"

"Ava, I found your stash of diaries. Every. Single. One."

"I LIKE TO READ THEM WHEN I'M HAVING A BAD DAY!" I shout. "They remind me that things could be worse, like the time I thought Panstick was an acceptable foundation or that blue eyeliner and Miss Sporty lip gloss was cool."

"O-KAY! I think that's enough for today," He holds out his hand, offering to help me off the floor.

Taking hold of his hand, he pulls, hiking me to my feet. "I agree. I'm tired, hungry, and in desperate need of all the alcohol. Besides, we need to order you a bed online. IKEA does home deliveries, right?"

"Avie, I am not ordering a bed from IKEA. I'd rather sleep on the floor."

"What have you got against IKEA? They have everything, even the things you didn't know you needed."

Danny gestures to himself, guiding his hand from the tip of his head down his body. "Do you see this? All six-foot-five inches of me."

"Erm, yes!" I'm confused. What's his height got to do with anything?

"Now, imagine me laying in a bed from IKEA."

I clamp my lips together, forcing back a laugh.

"Point made."

He brushes past me and stops in the doorway, flicking his gaze over his shoulder. "Besides, I need a bed with a solid frame," he winks. My inner walls clench, and my cheeks heat.

Hiding my all-too-blatant reaction, I decided to push back.

"Oh, yeah? And why's that?"

He smirks at me with his knicker disintegrator smile. "Maybe one day you'll find out."

My mouth drops to the floor, and the asshole laughs and exits the room as though he didn't just imply what I think he implied.

Clean up on aisle V. I repeat, clean up on aisle V.

IKEA, Causing Divorce Since 1943

DANNY

"I can't believe I let you talk me into this."

Ava smirks as she closes the passenger door of my Ford Ranger. The smile on her face *almost* makes the next three to six hours of torture worth it.

With a little too much pep in her step, Ava skips across the underground car park. She stuffs her hands into the pockets of her denim jacket, and she swings her arms backwards, turning it into a cape.

"I don't know why you're complaining," she shouts over her shoulder. "Everyone loves flat-packed furniture. The possibilities are endless — bookshelves, wardrobes, kitchens — you name it, IKEA has it."

Tilting my chin to the ceiling, I roll my eyes at her excitement and shout, "Nobody with a sane mind likes IKEA, Avie."

I catch up to her as she reaches the automatic doors in the centre of the underground. As we head for the elevator, she stops at the trolley bay to get a cart.

"We are not going to need that," I protest, knowing well if I let her, she will spend her life savings on pointless shit that she doesn't even need.

Ignoring me, she pushes the cart into the elevator and presses the button to the showrooms.

As we ascend, she turns to face me. "Did you know someone got married here?"

I raise my brow, wondering what the hell she's talking about. Who *the hell would get married in IKEA?*

"On that TV show *Don't Tell the Bride*," she continues. "It's on YouTube. I swear to God if my future husband was arranging my wedding, and he chose here — straight-up divorce."

I laugh at her outrage. "I thought you loved IKEA."

The doors open, and we step out into the tiny model apartments.

"I do. Oh, look at that rain shower," Ava waves to her right, then looks over her shoulder at me. "Does that mean I want to begin the rest of my life here? No, it does not."

"So, where would you like to get married?"

The question falls from my mouth, and there's not a thing I could have done to stop it.

"Hmm," she pounders. "I haven't put much thought into it, to be honest. All I know is I don't want a church wedding. Maybe a spiritual ceremony of some kind? What about you? Where does Daniel Peter O'Donoghue want to get hitched?"

I let my mind wander, and an image of me, standing under a familiar white gazebo waiting for my bride, flashes to the forefront of my mind. Plenty of men wouldn't give two shits about their wedding details, and up until this moment, I was one of those men.

I can't share my vision with her, though. Especially since the white gazebo in question is the same one we spent most of our childhood in, hidden between the trees at the bottom of Ava's parents' garden.

"I don't know," I lie. "Haven't thought about it either." *Lie, lie, lie.*

We spent the next two hours walking through the

showroom while Ava insists on checking every single cubby — God forbid she would miss something life-changing.

We spent the majority of our time in the bed section, arguing like a married couple. At one point, Ava storms off, leaving me standing there like a complete asshole while the other shop-goers shoot me dirty looks for upsetting what they probably assumed was my girlfriend or wife.

Finally, we make our way around the floor without killing each other, and Ava tells me there is another level.

IKEA, creating a better life for many people. What a load of bollox! IKEA causing divorce since 1943 seems more accurate.

"That was only the display part," she informs. "Now, we get to shop."

"What have we been doing all afternoon?"

"Browsing, Danny. We've been browsing."

"Luckily for you, I like you."

"You love me," she bats her lashes. "And you know it."

More than you know, Avie. More than you know.

"Do you *really* need more storage organisers?"

"Do I need them? No. Do I want them? Hell, yes! One can never have enough storage organisers. Have you learned nothing from The Home Edit?" Ava scoffs and continues to throw all different shapes of clear plastic into the trolley.

"Is that the show you made we watch on Netflix?"

"Yes! I follow them on Insta too. I'm obsessed with Clea and Joanna. I'd give my left tit for them to come and organise my apartment."

"You are the most unorganised person I ever met." I laugh as she holds up what looks like a sock drawer spacer.

"Exactly! They'd whip my ass, and I'd happily bend over and let them do it."

"What about me?" I tease.

"What about you?"

"Would you happily bend over and let me whip your ass?"

A blush creeps onto her cheeks, and her eyes go round. After a long, awkward pause, she shakes her head and replies, "I don't know how to answer that."

Suddenly, she spins on her heels, and following the ridiculous arrow system on the floor, she rushes towards the indoor plants.

A deep laugh that comes from the pit of my

stomach bursts free, and I shout after her. "That wasn't a no."

She continues her pursuit of indoor horticulture, but I don't miss the *'It wasn't a yes, either.'* that she throws over her shoulder.

Well, you can't blame a man for trying.

AFTER WASTING HOURS OF MY LIFE THAT I WILL NEVER get back, we finally make it back to the apartment.

"I can't believe you bought nothing." Ava twists the key into the lock as I trail behind her with far too many bags.

"Why are you so surprised? I told you, I am not, under any circumstances, buying a bed from IKEA."

"Fine, you win, but you're sleeping in my bed until we can order you a new one. You can't keep sleeping on this shitty couch."

If she wants me to sleep beside her, I won't protest. Last night was the best night's sleep I've had in I don't know how long. Probably because — unbeknownst to her — sleepy Ava spent the night curled up in my arms.

"I'll order one from Mattress Mick in the morning, but it might take a few days."

I follow her into the living room, place her purchases onto the floor, and flop down onto the couch. With my right hand, I rub my knee, massaging the tender ligaments.

Ava's face scrunches. "Is your knee still sore?"

"Yeah, a little."

She drops down on the couch beside me, and with maximum effort, lifts my legs onto her lap.

"I'm sorry. You should have said something. I wouldn't have dragged you shopping if you were in pain."

Shrugging my shoulder, I lay back against the arm of the couch. "I'm okay, honestly. It's just a little tender from walking on it. I'll be fine."

Her fingers needle into the swollen tissue, and my eyes close as I groan at the relief her touch brings. "Fuck, that feels amazing."

"Did Kye check this out for you? It feels very swollen."

Lifting my head slightly, I see the concern written all over her face — eyebrows furrowed, lips pulled into a tight line.

"Yeah, he examined it before I left the gym. He said I've more than likely sprained some ligaments and to rest up for a few days."

He also said not to go on any long walks or

anything that would cause overexertion. I leave out that piece of information, knowing that Ava will go crazy at me for ignoring Kye's physiotherapist orders.

"Hungry?" I ask, swiftly changing the subject. She side-eyes me but doesn't call me out.

"Yeah. I could eat. Do you want me to order some Chinese?"

"Sounds good."

We spend the rest of the night curled up on the couch, watching shitty shows, eating our body weight in fast food, and laughing at ridiculous TikTok videos before heading to bed. Finally, Ava falls asleep curled up against me, and it takes every ounce of willpower I have not to pull her in close and wrap my arms around her.

I gently push away the pale pink strands of her hair from her face with the tips of my fingers and watch her as she succumbs to sleep, her breaths deepening with every inhale. "I'm already yours, Avie. Tell me, what do I have to do to make you mine?"

Grab Hold Of Your Lady Balls

AVA

"Happy birthday to you. Happy Birthday to you. Happy birthday, dear Ava. Happy birthday to you."

"FUCK OFF!"

I pull the duvet over my head, blocking out the God-awful noise coming from Danny's mouth.

I am not, under any circumstances, leaving this bed.

If I get up now, I'll need to face the fact that I am a fully-fledged grown-up, and for that level of disappointment, I'm not equipped.

The bed slumps as Danny bounces onto my

mattress. Pulling the covers from me, he exposes me to the sunlight. Squeezing my eyes shut, I tell myself to stay fake-asleep. If I don't open my eyes, I can blissfully pretend that I am still in my prime and not three decades old.

I grapple with him, tugging at the blanket, but it's useless.

Fuck him and his massive man muscles.

"Go away. Leave me to wallow in pity."

His deep, gruff laughter fills the room as Danny chuckles at my resistance. "What if I told you I have birthday doughnuts?"

I freeze. *Did he say doughnuts?*

I roll over onto my stomach, avoiding the world by planting my face into my mattress, and mutter, "What kind of doughnuts?"

The mattress beneath me dips a little further, and a sudden heat covers my skin. Goosebumps rise on my bare legs, arms, and along the skin of my neck.

Suddenly his hot breath brushes over my ear, my inner thighs clench as he whispers, "You'll have to get up to find out."

My body stiffens beneath his, and I thank the Baba Jesus that he can't see the blush that has crept onto my cheeks.

What the hell is he doing, caging me beneath him like some sexual predator? Not that I mind, but that's a moot point.

Over the last week or so, Danny and I have fallen into a comfortable routine. It's been easy — well, for the most part. Sometimes, there seems to be this electric current that sparks between us, one I don't know how to deal with. So, instead of expressing my sudden need to mount my best friend, I tuck myself safely into a box of unawareness, keeping my feelings and my heart safe from destruction.

There have been times where I thought that maybe he was about to kiss me, but he'd always pull away at the last second, leaving me craving him like a fat kid craves cakes.

Every night, we would go to bed, and every morning I'd wake up cradled in his arms. We'd laugh it off, blaming our unconscious selves.

When Danny's bed arrived three days ago, and he moved into the other bedroom, I was a little disappointed.

Okay, so I was slightly devastated, but who are you to judge me? I am a grown woman with needs. Unfortunately for me, those needs involve my very off-limits bestie-slash-roommate and his giant, God-was-good-to-him cock. And no, I am not speculating. I've felt his Pleasure Pump pressing against my ass more times than it should, teasing me by knocking but never coming inside.

The barely-there brush of his fingers runs along the seam of my tank top, right over my ribcage, bringing me back to the present and causing me to hold my breath. "Don't make me tickle you, Avie."

I wiggle my ass a little, trying to knock him off me. I realise, all too quickly, that it was a terrible move on my part. He lifts himself slightly, giving me enough room to roll onto my back, of which I take full advantage.

Suddenly, we are face to face. A silence louder than any sound I've ever heard fills my bedroom. I take him in — a sharp, masculine nose framed by high cheekbones and perfect lips. Laughter lines dance around the corners of his glistening-with-mischief eyes, and the urge to lean forward, run my fingers through his slightly long hair, and capture his mouth with mine becomes intoxicating, flooding my every nerve-ending.

It's *the* look. Oh, you know the one. The look that passes between two people right before they kiss. It's a heart fluttering, lip trembling moment.

His brooding gaze drops to my lips, then he glances back up, hiding the fact that he's thinking about what it would feel like to take something we're not sure we should have.

It's a slow dance. The moment of the song right before the peaking crescendo, neither of us willing to break the unspoken rule of our friendship, yet both knowing that there's only one way this ends.

"Do it," my subconscious screams at me. "Grab hold of your lady balls and kiss him."

I close the distance between us and press my lips against his.

Danny's unexpected gasp is hushed by the sound of a lifetime of anticipation and what if's coming to a screeching halt. With a soft, uncertain touch, I brush my lips against his, waiting for permission, secretly hoping he will kiss me back.

I pull away, just enough to allow him to make the next move. Our eyes lock, and something unspoken burns in his irises — desire, want, need, all swirling together, rendering me speechless.

I've never felt anything like this before. It's as if Danny can see right through my eyes to somewhere deeper. Somewhere beyond my sassy, eclectic surface, and that terrifies me.

My heart thuds wildly in my chest, an erratic dance to the beat of anxiety whirling in the pit of my stomach.

Say something, my mind races, begging me to cut through the intense stare down.

Danny's hand touches my cheek as he rests his forehead against mine, holding my gaze in place.

I swallow, waiting for him to say something, do anything.

"Fuck it," he whispers against my mouth.

Suddenly he buries his hands in my hair, right at the nape of my neck, then he leans forward, caging me beneath him. Our lips collide in a needy, breathless kiss. I open for him, and he sweeps in, greedy for more.

The taste of spearmint, coffee, and something that's somehow uniquely Danny, erupts against my tongue. Together we get lost in each other — consequences be damned.

I savour each brush, lick, and taste as if it will be our last. At this moment, I don't care that I am kissing my best friend, and I don't worry about how irrevocably awkward it will be once we stop. I just embrace it.

The pace changes, deepening. Gone is the hesitation, and in its place is an insatiable hunger.

The bristles of Danny's beard scratches against my cheeks as our mouths work together in the most delicious way possible.

A soft hum falls from my lips as his hands roam under my tank top, setting my skin on fire.

Nobody has ever kissed me like this before. I'm floating, and there's not a thing that could drag me down from the high. It's not just a kiss — it's a hundred tiny moments and a million little touches, each one stealing another piece of my heart.

The apartment could fall down around me, and I wouldn't care, not one bit.

Suddenly, the doorbell rings and reality crashes down.

Danny pulls back, breaking our lust-filled spell. He leaps from the bed and buries his hands in his hair. His shoulders rise and fall as he catches his breath.

I lift myself onto my elbows and calm my breathing. I search his face for a reaction, and I don't like what I see — wide eyes, full of regret.

"Shit," he mutters. "I shouldn't have…FUCK!"

The doorbell sounds again, and I want to murder the culprit.

Before I can muster a response, he turns on his heel and flees the room.

"Danny!" I call out.

In the distance, his bedroom door slams, and I bury my face into my palms.

My heart sinks like the Titanic to the bottom of my stomach, but somehow, I manage to halt myself from the bed.

Scurrying down the hallway, I open the door to find Charlie on the other side, holding a bouquet of unicorn and doughnut balloons.

"HAPPY BIRTHDAY!" she shouts.

Finally, she looks at me, and her happy-go-lucky mood vanishes.

"Uh-oh! What happened?"

I shake my head, silently telling her *not now*. She nods in understanding as I hold out my arm, motioning for her to come in. Silently, she follows me down the hall towards my bedroom.

Once we're inside the safety of my room, she tries again.

"What's wrong, Avie? Did something happen?"

Pulling clothes from my wardrobe, I look over my shoulder. "I can't right now. Let me get dressed, and we can go to The Rusty Spoon."

She looks toward my bedroom door, and I know she's silently asking if my not-so-happy face has anything to do with Danny.

"Not here," I repeat.

"Fine. But don't think you're getting out of telling me."

"I know, but I need to gather my thoughts. Somewhere far away from here."

Her eyes widen. "That bad, huh?"

"Worse," I confirm.

Much-fucking-worse.

Put Your Gloves Up Or Take Them Off

DANNY

WHEN AVA HIGH-TAILED IT FROM THE APARTMENT with Charlie, I took a baltic blue-ball-killer shower, which did nothing to dull the ache, then I grabbed my gym bag and headed for the gym.

I have strict orders from Kye to stay off my knee, but I need to clear my head, and the only way I know how is to sweat it out — so, here I am, at Game On Fitness.

My fists hit the bag with vicious frustration, and with every jab, I release all the pent-up energy and tension.

What the hell was I thinking?

You know what, don't answer that. I wasn't thinking, not at all.

I fucked up, big style.

That kiss, fuck, that kiss was the best kiss of my life, and what did I do? I fucking ran because it scared the ever-loving shit out of me.

Every ounce of my self-control demolished by one brush of her lips. Then, like a raving lunatic, I attacked her as though I was a starved man who got presented a gourmet meal.

For years, I buried the urge, promising myself I'd never risk our friendship by crossing the invisible line we created.

Deep down, I always knew kissing Ava would be spectacular. But fuck me, I was not prepared for my heart to bounce right out of my chest and land in the palm of her hands.

Her lips were sweeter than I ever imagined they'd be. If Charlie hadn't interrupted, I wouldn't have stopped, not until Ava was naked, trembling beneath me with the after-effects of her release.

I was lost after one taste of her lips but found again after one touch of her skin, leaving zero doubt in my mind that Ava McCann could never belong to anyone else. She is mine. The only question is, how the fuck do we do this without fucking it all up?

Lost in thought, I don't spot Kye coming up behind me.

"What are you doing here? You're supposed to be resting your knee. It won't heal itself."

Ignoring him, I continue to pound the bag.

I shouldn't have kissed her like that. I fought it, for years, the battle between my head and my heart. And now, I'm pissed — no, terrified, cause I'm pretty sure I have ruined a lifelong friendship.

Kye's hand lands on my shoulder, halting me.

"What the hell has gotten into you? Your fight is in three weeks, D. You need to rest your leg, or you'll be toast before the end of the first round."

My shoulders slump. Kye is right. What good would it do if I caused more damage to my already banjaxed knee?

Lifting my wrist to my mouth, I use my teeth to pull open the velcro securing my hand wrap and unravel my knuckles and wrists.

"Sorry, I have a lot on my mind."

"Next time call me. You don't need to act recklessly. You only get one shot at this, Danny. You can't afford to fuck it up. If you need to talk, I'm here."

One look at my little brother and the guilt sweeps in, nearly knocking me off my feet.

We grew up in this gym, and unlike Keegan — who took after our ma — Kye and I ate and slept MMA.

Together we'd planned to take the UFC by storm. Unfortunately, with a nasty kick to the head, Kye lost some vision in his left eye, putting an end to his career.

I sit on the mat and pat the space beside me, silently asking Kye to join me. He drops down and holds out a bottle of unopened water.

"Here," he states.

I twist the lid off and bring it to my lips, swallowing down half the bottle in two gulps.

Finally, Kye breaks the silence. "So, Danny boy, what got you so wound up?"

I raise my knees, drawing them up to my chest, then settle my elbows on top.

Releasing a sigh, I pick at the label on the bottle. "Avie and I kissed."

He whistles out his shock. "Shit. I was not expecting that. I mean, I'm not surprised, but why are you caught up about it? Was it awful or something?"

I place the water bottle on the mat, lift my hand

to my head, and bury my fingers in my fringe, brushing the sweat-soaked strands from my eyes. "No!" I sigh. "It was the best fucking kiss of my life, but it's Avie."

"So what! You've loved that girl your whole life. You should be over the moon, not moping around the gym. What happened?"

I think back to this morning, to the moment I entered Ava's room. When I ripped the covers off her, I was not expecting to find her half-naked — nipples standing at full attention, her perfect buds peeking through the thin material of her tank-top.

I almost came on the spot.

"Honest answer? I have no idea. One minute I'm singing happy birthday, and the next, I'm tonsils deep. She was staring at me with her big doe eyes, and then, we were going at it like two horney teenagers at the back of a movie theatre."

Kyle runs his tongue across his bottom lip, and his eyes crinkle. "Don't take this the wrong way... but how did you go from kissing the girl of your wet dreams to pounding a boxing bag? What am I missing here?"

I huff, exhaling a heavy breath out my nose. "I called Charlie last night and asked her to distract Ava today so that I could organise Ava's surprise party.

She showed up right at the wrong time and put a stop to our morning make-out session."

"Shit."

"Yeah! And that's not even the worst part. When Ava and I pulled apart, she looked horrified. Like she'd just made the biggest mistake of her life. So I bolted."

Kye blinks at my stupidity. "What do you mean you bolted?"

Dragging my hands over my face, I relive the moment all over again. Kye stares at me as if I've lost my mind. And honestly, it feels like I have.

"You," he draws out. "are an idiot!"

"I know."

"What now?"

"I have no idea. I don't want to ruin Avie's surprise party." I reply. "But I'll have to talk to her at some point. It's not like we can pretend it didn't happen."

He nods his head as his eyes dart from side to side in thought. Finally, he says, "You need to ignore the enormous-T-REX in the room, if only for tonight. Then tomorrow, you find your balls and tell her how you feel."

"It's not that simple," I protest.

Using his palms, he pushes off the mat and jumps

to his feet. He looks down at me and holds out his hand to pull me up. Once I'm on my feet, he states, "It is, D. Either put your gloves up or take them off. Opportunity only knocks once. Don't be a fool. Open the fucking door."

After my conversation with Kye, I head to the changing rooms. I pull my bag from the locker and remove my phone.

The screen lights up, highlighting six messages from Charlie.

Charlie: Hey, Hot Lips! I'm all for morning make-out sessions, really I am, but for fucks sake, D. Why today?

Charlie: Oh, never mind! She kissed you first, my mistake.

Charlie: You ran?? WTF! I swear to the devil worshipers, I need to bang your heads together.

Charlie: Stop ignoring me, Mountain Man! I'm in the middle of a level five meltdown. How do you expect me to get her to the party with the mood she's in? Huh?

Charlie: Why are all men idiots?

Charlie: Daniel O'Donoghue, answer me! If this surprise party — that we've spent weeks planning — goes to pot, I am blaming you; you overgrown, kiss and run gobshite. So help me, I will cut your balls off and feed them to my neighbours' chickens.

Danny: Calm down, Half Pint! Everything will be fine. I'll fix it, I promise. All you need to do is get her to The Rink for eight. Leave the rest to me.

Charlie: DANNY?

Danny: Yeah?

Charlie: DON'T FUCK THIS UP!

Danny: I won't.

Everything Great Was Made In The 90s

AVA

"CAN YOU PUT THE PHONE DOWN FOR TWO SECONDS? I am in the middle of a life crisis here."

Charlie lays her iPhone on the table with the screen faced down. She pulls her strawberry milkshake towards her and wraps her glossy lips around the straw.

Finally, she looks up at me, giving me her full attention. "I don't see what the big deal is. So, you kissed your best friend. It's not as though you didn't want to."

Placing my elbows on the table, I cup my cheeks in my palms and release a frustrated breath.

"It is a massive deal. You didn't see him, Charlie. He hightailed it out of there like The Road Runner."

"I think we need a man's opinion on this." Lifting her arms high in the air, she flaps them around like she's at an open-air rave.

I reach across the table and pull at her forearms, trying to calm her before she draws any unwanted attention.

"Would you stop," she swipes. "Keegan, woo-hoo, over here."

"Oh, hey, Charlie." He responds. Changing his direction, he approaches our table.

I raise my hand to cover my eyes as embarrassment colours my cheeks. "Why are we friends?"

Keegan slides into the seat next to me. "Happy Birthday, Cee-Cee. The big three-o!"

"Don't remind me," I grumble.

His brown eyes — so similar to his brothers' — flick between Charlie and me. "What are you lovely ladies doing today? Have you any celebratory plans?"

Charlie pipes up, looking a little shifty for my liking. "Nope! Nothing crazy."

She nods her head in my direction. "Ava here

would rather deny the fact that she has hit three decades young."

"I'm sure it's not that bad," he laughs.

"Says the guy who owns a restaurant at the age of twenty-eight."

"I was twenty-six when I opened this place, but who am I to brag." His lips curl into a sparkling smile, one that would melt the knickers of most ladies. Not me though, there's only one man that could have me naked by flashing me his dimples, and unfortunately, Keegan is not him.

"So," he adds. "What's happening?"

Charlie leans forward, and I shoot her a don't-you-dare look. Which she blatantly ignores.

"Ava kissed Danny."

Keegan's head flies back as laughter erupts from his mouth.

When neither Charlie nor I join in, he sits forward.

"Oh, you're not joking!"

Leaning forward, I bang my head on the table, wishing I could rewind to this morning and take back the split-second decision I made to lock lips with my best friend.

"Unfortunately not!" I mutter.

Slowly, I raise my head, side-eyeing them as they bask in my misery.

Keegan is silent for a moment, then he holds his hand out, and Charlie plonks a fifty euro note into his palm. "Thank you."

"Bite me," she responds before crossing her arms over her chest like a scolded child.

"What was that?" I sit up straight, waving my hand between the two of them.

Keegan's lips curl up into a shit-eating grin. "We had a bet."

"You're unbelievable. I can't deal with you two."

"Don't blame us for being the last two standing," Charlie shrugs her shoulders.

My eyes widen into saucers. "What do you mean, the last two?"

Keegan sits back into his seat and tilts his head toward me. "Oh, everyone is in on this — have been for years. I think our ma's started it around the time you turned twenty-one."

"Seriously?" I baulk at the audacity.

"Oh, yeah. My ma was the first to lose," Keegan informs me. "She was convinced Danny was going to make his move at your twenty-first."

Lifting her hand above the table, Charlie spreads her fingers and uses them to list the people involved. "Mammy McCann said twenty-five. Suzie picked twenty-six. Kye said twenty-eight. And me and wannabe Gordon Ramsey, here, both chose thirty."

Unbelievable! Why am I friends with these people?

"If you both picked thirty, why did you pay him?"

"Oh, we had a side bet," Charlie adds as if it's no big deal. "Who would kiss who?"

"And you picked me?" My eyes lock on Keegan.

"Seemed like the obvious choice. Don't get me wrong, Danny has had a massive boner for you for years, but I knew he'd never make the first move."

"Oh my Christ! What is wrong with all of you? He's my best friend! We were not meant to be kissing each other, ever. It was a bad lapse of judgment on my part, one I will never get over. I swear on my life, I have never been so embarrassed. Friends don't kiss friends."

The rise of Keegan's eyebrow makes me want to slam the oh-really look off his face.

"You're right. Friends don't kiss friends," he states. "I'd never kiss Charlie. Never even thought about it, to be honest."

"Hey! That's rude." Her hand clutches her chest. "I'm a fantastic kisser. You'd be lucky to lock lips with me."

"Oh, shut up." His gaze flashes to Charlie. "It's not like you ever imagined me naked either."

"True," She shrugs, then takes another sip of her milkshake.

Keegan focuses back on me. "My point is you and Danny are more than friends, Cee-Cee. Always have been."

"Of course we are. I love him. We've been friends forever, Keegan."

I'm clutching at straws, and he knows it.

"True. You have known each other forever. You've also known Kye and me our whole lives, but you don't want to jump our bones, do you?"

No! I silently reply, knowing all too well he has a point.

Danny, Keegan, and Kye have always been in my life, but I don't feel anything for either of the younger O'Donoghue brothers — only friendship.

I've never imagined either one of them naked while doing the downtown tango with Victor the Vibrator. I've never pictured what my future would look like if it were one of them by my side — only Danny.

Fucked! I am totally and utterly fucked!

"I'll take your silence as validation. You don't just love my brother, Cee-Cee. You're in love with him."

My fingers pick at the menu on the table. Avoiding Keegan's eyes, I mutter, "What does it matter anyway? He doesn't feel the same way. If he did, he wouldn't have fled the room like his pants had gone up in flames."

"If I know my brother the way I think I do, he's just as wound up about what happened as you are. Give him some time. Let him stew on his thoughts. He loves you, Cee-Cee. There's no doubt about it." Keegan rises from his seat, places his hands flat on the table, and leans forward.

"So, French toast?" He changes the subject, which I appreciate.

"Extra bacon?"

"You bet! Anything for my future sister-in-law," he adds, turning on his heel and laughing all the way to the kitchen.

"Jackass," I shout after him, making him laugh louder.

"Do I really need to wear this ridiculous blindfold?"

After we left The Rusty Spoon, Charlie and I headed to the salon, where I received a birthday blow-dry and a full face of make-up from Jen, the in-house make-up artist.

Finally, after a total it's-my-birthday makeover, Charlie handed me what she dubbed my must-wear birthday outfit.

Now, here I am, in the front of her hot pink Volkswagen Beetle wearing the shortest pair of pink shorts I've ever worn, paired with white knee-high socks, a pink and white striped cropped top that shows off my midriff, an oversized denim jacket and a unicorn horn headband.

"Yes! Otherwise, you'll ruin the surprise."

"I don't like surprises. Besides, I don't want a party. I want my onesie, the tv remote, and a share box of doughnuts."

"You do that every night. It's a big birthday, Ava. You need to celebrate it. So, quit your moaning. We're almost there."

"And where is there?"

I can't see her, but I know she's rolling her eyes because the radio volume turns up, drowning out my are-we-there-yet commentary.

Finally, after what feels like a life sentence, the car comes to a stop.

"Can I take this off?

"No!"

I hear the click of her door opening. A few seconds pass, then the passenger door opens, and a cool breeze hits my bare legs.

"Hands, please."

I hold out my hands, and Charlie takes hold and guides me out of my seat.

My feet hit the hard ground, and Charlie links our elbows, walking us both forward.

My head swivels around as I try to listen to the sounds around me, but I'm met by silence.

Where the hell are we?

"When can I remove this blindfold?"

"Two more minutes, we're almost there. Don't worry, I won't let you walk into anything," Charlie laughs, doing nothing for my confidence.

"You'd better not."

We come to a stop, and a rush of heat hits me.

"Okay, you need to step inside. There are three steps, then a doorway."

Concentrating, I follow her instructions.

I hope nobody is watching this cause I'm betting I look ridiculous.

Suddenly the electro sound of *Up & Down* by Vengaboys assaults my ears. The music is so loud, I can barely hear myself think.

A laugh bursts from my mouth. "What the fuck? Did I step into a time machine?"

"You might as well have!" I know that voice — deep and gruff, like vocal porn to my Lady Lunchbox.

Danny O'Donoghue.

Rough fingertips brush against my cheeks, carefully lifting the blindfold from my eyes and giving me a close-up view of his devilishly handsome face.

"Happy Birthday, Avie."

The shy smile on his face is hypnotic. Danny is usually so sure of himself, but it seems he's somewhat hesitant after our little tongue tango this morning.

It takes a hot minute for my eyes to adjust to the flashing disco lights, but I recognise where I am once they do.

"The Rink!" I squeal with excitement.

Danny and I spent half of our childhood here, only solidifying my love for all things from the naughty nineties.

Peeking over his shoulder, I spy my friends, co-workers, and family members standing on the polished hardwood roller skating rink. Two massive neon painted signs are hung along the wall of the rink. One reading *'Ava Turns Thirty'*, and the other stating *'Everything great was made in the 90's'*.

Flicking my eyes back to Danny, I flash him a smile that reaches my eyes. "This is so awesome. Did you do all this?"

He shrugs his shoulders as if it isn't a big deal. "Ahh, I had some help."

Scanning the room, I take it all in. Assorted balloons decorate every corner in all different shapes and sizes — The old MTV logo, unicorns, and doughnuts.

Cardboard pastel-coloured shapes hang from the ceiling giving the place a retro feel, and don't get me started on the Saved by The Bell themed photobooth because I'd be here all night.

"It's amazing, D. Thank you." Before I realise what I'm doing, my arms loop around his neck and my lips land on his cheek.

His larger-than-life body stiffens, and I pull back, but his arms circle my waist, keeping me pressed against his chest.

"I wanted to have all your favourite things in one place. Roller skates, doughnuts, unicorns, and the nineties."

Tilting my chin, I stare into his mesmerising eyes. "I love it!"

And I love you!

Thankfully, I keep that last part to myself.

The Running Man On Skates

DANNY

"What, in the name of God, are you wearing?" Laughter dances around her eyes. Ava scans me from head to toe, taking in my skin-tight white tee, ripped light denim jeans, and my sleeveless jean jacket.

"It's a nineties-themed party. Can't be the nineties without double denim."

A slow smile hides at the corners of her lips. "Well, you did a good job. You're looking very David Charvet, circa Baywatch."

"Is that a compliment?" I tease, knowing well,

Ava had a giant-ass poster of him over her bed for years. Obsessed is an understatement.

"Take it however you like," she winks, and it sends shockwaves of want straight to my dick.

She looks around, taking everything in, and I can't help the excitement that swells in my chest. I know she said she didn't want a party, but sometimes, I know her better than she knows herself.

"How did you rent this whole place? Enda doesn't usually do private parties."

"For you, Enda insisted. She watched us grow up in this rink, and when I asked her if we could rent the place, she was more than happy to oblige — well," I laugh. "as long as she got an invite."

"It's amazing, D. Thank you so much for doing this for me. I love it so much."

"You're welcome. Besides, I couldn't think of a better way for you to enter adulthood then reliving your childhood."

"Come on," I link her arm with mine. "Let's get you some skates, and then we can say hello to everyone."

Mischief takes over her face, and instantly I know what she's thinking.

"Race you," she shouts as she takes off towards the skate rental area.

I STAND AT THE EDGE OF THE ROLLER-SKATING RINK watching as Ava spins around the maple hardwood floor to every cheesy nineties-song you can imagine. If the broad smile on her face tells me anything, it's that she's thoroughly enjoying tonight, just like I hoped she would.

We still haven't spoken about what happened this morning, but that hasn't stopped me from thinking about it every time her smiley eyes meet mine.

It's taking every ounce of strength I have not to wrap my arms around her waist, pull her in close, and claim her lips with mine.

Watching her float around the dancefloor in those tiny pink shorts is driving me crazy.

The song switches to *C'est la Vie* by Bewitched, and Ava and Charlie break into a ridiculous dance. At one point, Charlie attempts an Irish jig, resulting in her landing on her ass in a fit of laughter.

"What are you doing over here by yourself?"

Peering over my shoulder, I find my mother watching me with a curious look in her eyes.

She stands beside me and looks up to scan my face. "What's going on in that head of yours, boy?"

Without realising it, my gaze flicks towards Ava.

"Ah, I see," she smiles.

Deciding to play dumb, I ask, "See what?"

She shakes her head, adding in an eye roll, then tilts her head to the ceiling. "Lord, if you can hear me, please tell me why my son is behaving like an idiot?"

I raise my brows. "Very funny, Ma!"

Lifting her hand, she lightly slaps my arm. "I'm not joking, Daniel. Everyone in this building knows you love that girl," she tips her head in Ava's direction. "Everyone, except her."

"She knows I care about her."

The look she gives me transports me back to my teenage years. It's the one a mother gives you when she knows you're full of shit — chin tilted to the side, brows raised, and let's not forget the pursed lips.

"Of course, she knows you care, but she can't read your mind, son. Don't lose her to some asshole because you're too chicken-shit to tell her you love her."

"I won't."

"Really?" She points to the dance floor. I follow her finger, and my heart almost falls out of my ass.

Right there, in the middle of the rink, Cathal Daly has his hands in Ava's as she drags him around the dance floor. They're laughing at something, and the feeling that explodes under my skin is anything but pleasant. I should never have let Charlie invite him.

I've never been the jealous type, but recently that has changed, and I'd be lying if I said it had nothing to do with my pink-haired best friend.

Ava never did talk about how her date with Cathal went but seeing them together makes my blood pressure rise.

"Jealousy is not a good look on you," my ma states.

"I'm not jealous."

"Yeah, and I'm Oprah."

"No, you're annoying," I flash her a smile, softening my insult.

"Har har! Now, quit your moping and go get your girl."

"I can't. Kye banned me from skating because of my knee."

"You leave him to me. Go, have fun, and for the love of my future grandbabies, tell the girl you love her."

With that, she walks off, leaving me to decipher my thoughts.

"Fuck it!"

Laced up and ready to go, I step onto the rink. It's been a few years since I was last on this floor, but it all comes back as soon as I push off the wall.

"Easy," I think. Like riding a bike.

My eyes lock on Ava, Charlie, Cathal, and Keegan, and I head for the rink's centre. "Mind if I steal the birthday girl?"

"Danny! You're here. I thought you couldn't skate with your knee?" Ava beams.

"One dance won't hurt, right?" I hold out my hand, and without hesitation, she takes it.

Suddenly, the song switches mid-track, and I know my meddling mother had something to do with it. "I swear to fuck, one day soon, I will put that woman in a home," I mutter beneath my breath.

Ava's laughter erupts from her bright pink lips. I know what she's thinking, and it is not happening.

She narrows her bright blue eyes and bats those hypnotising lashes that make it hard for me to say no.

"Not happening," I protest.

"Ah, please, D. It's my birthday."

I draw in a deep breath and blow it out through my nose. "Fine. But, for the record, your birthday is the only reason I'm reliving the most embarrassing moment of my life.

Ava squeals as she raises her hand, silently asking the DJ to restart the track.

"Kill me now."

The tell-tale opening bassline of *Ice, Ice Baby* blasts through the speakers, and Ava and I break into the well-known dance routine made famous by none other than Vanilla Ice.

Everybody stops, and suddenly all eyes are on us as we break it down like it's 1990 all over again.

Have you ever tried to do The Running Man on skates? How about The Scissors or The Roger Rabbit? There's no doubt about it, we look insane, but the joy that's radiating from Ava makes every second worth it.

Finally, after making a complete idiot out of myself, Ava does a double twist, landing right in my arms, knocking me off balance. Everyone cheers while Ava and I land on the floor in a hysterical heap.

We lie there, on our backs, staring at the ceiling. After a second, we turn our heads and look at each other.

"I can't believe we remembered how to do that," she chuckles, her shoulders shaking with laughter.

"Seriously? You made me practise that dance for months. Of course, I remember it."

Reaching over, I brush the hair off her face. "Happy Birthday, Avie."

Her tongue peeks out, roaming over her bottom lips, and the urge to kiss her becomes unbearable.

Shifting forward, I push up on my palms, then hold out my hand to help her up off the floor.

"Come on." I pull her to her feet. "I have one more surprise for you. You haven't even seen the best part yet."

Excitement rises on her gorgeous face, lighting up her eyes and widening her smile.

"There's more?"

I pull Ava off the rink towards the side door that leads out to the rear car park with her hand in mine. "Prepare yourself, Avie. You ain't seen nothing yet."

"I don't know what could be better than this. Tonight has been amazing." Her eyes bounce around the skating rink.

We quickly remove our skates, then I push open the heavy metal door and focus on Ava's face, not wanting to miss a second of her reaction.

Her hand flies from my hold to her mouth, masking her shock. "Is that... Oh, my God! Where did you get it? Can I go on it? Best day. EVER!"

I throw my head back, laughing at her childlike reaction. If I knew this was all it took to make her smile like the world was hers, I would have done it years ago.

"Of course, you can go on it. It's for you."

She takes off running, then hops up onto the heavy-duty nylon and bounces up onto the mechanical ride.

Swinging her legs over, she sits onto the saddle. "I cannot believe you got me a mechanical unicorn. Where in the world did you find this?"

"This is Darragh. He is a member of Da's gym. He rents these out for birthday parties. When I heard he had a unicorn, I had to get it for you."

Darragh presses a few buttons, and suddenly Ava is squealing like a five-year-old on Christmas morning.

I lean against the edge, watching her beaming face with pride.

When the ride finishes, she bounds off it and barrels straight into me. Her legs lock around my waist as she steadies herself by wrapping her arms around my neck.

"Danny O'Donoghue, you are the most ah-mazing person I've ever met."

Her lips pepper kisses all over my face. "Thank you. Thank you. Thank you."

I pull back slightly, taking in every inch of her face.

"Anything to make you smile, Avie. Absolutely anything."

What If It's You, Avie?

AVA

"Are you looking at my ass?" I giggle, just a little tipsy from the few cocktails I had at The Rink.

Stopping mid-stride, I look over my shoulder at Danny, who is climbing the stairway to our apartment behind me.

"I can't help it. Those are the tiniest pair of shorts I've ever seen. With every step you take, your ass cheeks wave at me."

"Well, it's rude to stare. Especially if you're not willing to follow up with a grope."

He raises his brow and hits me with a smouldering look. "Who says I'm not willing?"

I shrug my shoulder. "I don't see anyone stopping you."

Something dark and dangerous sparkles in his eyes and I'd be lying if I said I didn't want to explore it. But in true Danny fashion, he keeps his thoughts to himself and responds with a smirk.

Finally, we reach the door of our apartment. Danny unlocks it, pushing it open and motioning for me to enter first.

I can honestly say I have never had as much fun as I did tonight.

I have finally realised that turning thirty is not so bad.

After all, thirty is only a number, and no matter how old I get, it's okay to act like a kid from time-to-time. Just because I've come to a point in life where bills, jobs, and adult responsibilities are at the forefront of my daily to-do list doesn't mean I should stop believing in magic.

I still can't get over everything he planned tonight — every detail, perfectly chosen to showcase everything I love in life.

It just goes to show how well he knows me —

each slightly loopy part, and somehow, he still sticks around, basking in all my crazy.

My ever-growing feelings for him are becoming harder and harder to ignore. Making me wonder if telling him how I feel is such a bad thing.

I know he cares about me. After everything he did to make tonight memorable, how could he not?

Then the horror that was this morning plays on repeat in the back of my mind, making me question everything.

I'm not stupid! I'm fully aware Danny will forever be my white knight, riding in on his white horse and stealing the breath from my lungs.

There isn't a man on this earth who could compete with him when it comes to my heart. He owns it, whether he's aware of that fact or not.

I need to decide whether I want to risk our friendship over the possibility of what could be. In ten years, would I regret hiding my feelings? Could I watch him marry someone else?

Using the wall for support, I lean down and unlace my high-top converse.

"Not tonight," I think to myself.

"Something wrong?" Danny interrupts my thoughts. "You're thinking awfully loud."

Placing my shoes on the shoe rack, I turn to face him and nearly swallow my tongue.

There I go again, enjoying another eye orgasm.

Propped up against the wall with his tattooed forearms crossed over his broad chest, Danny strips me bare, with just a look.

Fuck a duck!

Why does he look so good in a plain white tee and double denim? It shouldn't be possible — yet here we are.

I blink back the X-rated images that have me hot-and-definitely-bothered and finally reply, "How does one think loud?"

Kicking off the wall, he closes the distance between us.

My heart pounds a little faster, and with every step he takes, the look in his deep brown eyes steals my mobility.

When there isn't an inch of space left between us, Danny lifts his hand. Picking up a strand of my hair, he twirls it around his finger. "Did you enjoy your birthday, Avie?"

Has anyone seen my tongue? I seemed to have lost it!

Nodding as a reply, I hold his gaze.

His eyes are hypnotic, and I can't look away, even if I wanted to.

"About this morning —"

Somehow, I find my tongue and cut him off. "Don't worry about it. I don't know what I was thinking. I should never have kissed you."

"I'm glad you did."

Sorry, what? Did I hear him right?

"Don't look so surprised." His shoulders rise, and a slight throaty chuckle escapes him. "Avie, I am done running from this. I've spent most of my life, avoiding what I feel for you. Doing whatever the fuck I could to keep you tucked safely in the friend zone because I was terrified you didn't feel the same."

"I —"

Danny lifts his finger to my lips, silencing me.

"Hear me out first, okay?"

"Okay."

"When you kissed me this morning, I knew. I knew no matter how fucking fast I tried to run away from my feelings — I'd only be running from the inevitable. Nobody can ever compare to you. You're the girl who stole my heart when I was too young to realise you even took it. Believe me; over the years, I've tried so many times to make my relationships work, but what if it's you, Avie? What if it's always ever going to be you."

My ears are ringing, and the weight of his words sit heavy on my chest, making it hard to breathe.

This is not a conversation we should be having standing in the middle of my tiny hallway, but I don't think it's right to call him out for his timing after what he just shared.

The point is, he wants this, whatever this is, and somehow that is even more terrifying than — I don't know — something truly fucking scary.

"So, you didn't hate kissing me?"

Honestly, Ava? Could you have asked a more idiotic question?

He cups my flaming hot cheeks in his hands, his eyes never wavering from mine.

"I didn't hate kissing you."

My awkward self decides now is the perfect time to rear her unwanted head. "Okay, well that's good to know, you know for next time. Not that I'm assuming there's going to be a next time."

He sniggers.

"I should probably stop talking now cause I'm only —"

Holy hot lips on mine!

The force of his lips meeting mine almost knocks me off my feet, but he holds me steady, gently clutching my face in his palms. Using his thumbs, he tilts my chin slightly, deepening our connection and, holy fuck, sensory overload!

I feel it everywhere, consuming me like wildfire, burning into my memory, never to be forgotten for the rest of my life.

I breathe him in, and his signature scent of sandalwood, vetiver, and cedar fills my nose.

Shockwaves of desire flood my body, and everything around me fades. There's no more holding back.

I always wondered what the difference between kissing someone else and kissing Danny would feel like — it turns out the former ends the moment my lips part, and the latter will stay with me until the end of time.

I wrap my arms around his neck as his hands travel past the material of my cropped top, igniting goosebumps along the bare skin above the waistband of my shorts.

I'm greedy, desperately craving more.

Suddenly his hands grip my ass, lifting me off my feet. I wrap my legs around his waist, holding myself steady as he devours me with each brush of his tongue.

He pulls back slightly before burying his face in

my neck. "Fuck, Ava." His words dance across my skin, sending a shock of want through my core.

My nipples pebble, brushing against the material of my top. My hands grip the back of his shirt, and I tear at the fabric, needing it gone.

Danny shifts me to the right, and with his free hand, he reaches back, and tugs the white tee over his head, then drops it on the floor.

Fuck me, that was seriously hot!

Without taking his eyes off mine, Danny walks toward my bedroom and kicks the door open with his foot.

"Tell me to stop," he whispers against my lips.

"What if I don't want you to?"

My back hits the mattress with a soft thud, and Danny cages me beneath him.

"I don't want you to wake up in the morning and regret this. You need to be sure."

Sliding my left hand into the hair at the nape of his neck, I draw him closer. "I will never regret a single moment with you."

His fingers trace my ribcage, delicately roaming over my cherry blossom tattoo.

"I love this," he whispers against my collarbone. "I still remember the day you got it. You looked so beautiful. When the tattoo artist asked for your number, I wanted to punch him straight in the dick."

A laugh rumbles from my chest. "Says the guy who kissed the receptionist only mere minutes before. He would never have asked for my number before that. He thought we were a couple until you played tonsil hockey with — what was her name again? Oh, yeah, Delilah!"

"Avie?"

"Yes!"

"Stop talking."

I nod my head for him to proceed. "As you were."

He shakes his head, brushing off his amusement while his fingers grip the edge of my top. I lean forward slightly, and he lifts it over my head.

"So. Fucking. Beautiful."

Dipping his head, he runs his tongue over my pert nipple. The hum that travels up his throat makes my hips lift from the bed.

My hands roam over his taut back muscles, stopping at the waistband of his jeans.

"Off!" I demand, and he's eager to oblige.

Next to go are my shorts, and thankfully he doesn't comment on my somewhat cute but most definitely not fuck-me-sexy, pink polka dot thong.

I shift my hips as he guides them down my legs.

Once they're off, he flings them over his shoulder, and they land somewhere amidst the rest of my floordrobe.

Both naked and needy, we become a flurry of kisses and touches as we make up for a lifetime of anticipation.

"So fucking long," his rough stubble grazes my inner thigh. "I've waited so fucking long to taste you."

Without warning, his tongue runs along my slit, and my inner walls tighten in appreciation. My hands dive into his unruly hair, gripping it as he feasts on me like a starved caveman.

He licks my clit with just the right amount of pressure, and my back arches, my body silently pleading for more.

I never knew it could feel like this. My body is seconds away from imploding, every nerve pulsating at each brush, lick, and flick of his tongue.

"More," I cry out, chasing the high he is so willing to give me.

"There. OH, MY GOD! Right there!"

Hands On The Headboard

DANNY

Ava erupts on my tongue; her orgasm ripples through her body, leaving her a beautiful, quivering mess beneath me.

Never in my life have I seen a more stunning sight.

Her body quakes from the pleasure of her release, making me question why it took so long for us to get to this point?

Conclusion: I am an idiot.

My hand skims her thigh, my fingers dancing

delicately in the crevice where her hip dips into her centre.

A visible shudder floods her body, and a throaty moan falls from her swollen lips.

Her hair fans over her pillow in a wild mess of pink and blue strands. She looks stunning, cheeks flushed from her orgasm.

I dot tiny butterfly kisses along the bare skin of her stomach, leaving no inch of her midriff untouched by my lips.

Her hands roam over my shoulders and down my arms, tracing my tattoos.

I kiss my way up her chest, allowing my breath to tickle her skin. Her back arches, forcing her chest to rise, teasing me.

I bring my head to her chest, and my tongue sweeps across her nipple. She trembles in my arms, riding out the wave.

"Jesus, Avie. You look so beautiful when you come."

Her hands are everywhere, her nails digging into my back.

"Danny! I need you."

I don't have a condom. Shit!

"Ava, I don't —"

"It's okay." It's as if she can read my thoughts.

"I'm on the pill."

"Are you sure? I'm clean. We get tested regularly at the gym."

Her tongue runs across my collarbone. "I'm positive. Fuck me like you've been dreaming about it all your adult life."

Oh, I intend to.

My hands grip her waist, lifting her off the mattress, and in one swift motion, I flip her onto her stomach before pulling her hips back, ass in the air.

"Hands on the headboard, Avie."

Her hands grip the headboard, and she peers over her shoulder. Her cobalt blue eyes pierce through me, and the devilish smile on her flawless face almost has me coming undone.

"Last chance to back out," I offer, rubbing the tip of my cock over her entrance.

"The only thing I'm backing on to is your dick."

Ava has always had a way with words, so it doesn't surprise me that her lack of filter carries over to the bedroom.

Not that I'm complaining. I love a girl who knows what she wants and needs when it comes to sex.

Shifting my hips forward, I sink into her. And fucking hell. I see stars.

"So fucking tight."

"God, yes! deeper!"

I hold her in place with my right hand while my left glides up her spine and takes hold of her long hair. I tug, pulling her head back slightly, elongating her neck. With each thrust, her back arches, and I sink deeper into her bliss.

Over and over, I pound into her. Her ass slaps against my lower stomach, and her beautiful tits bounce with every plunge.

"Danny." My name falls from her lips, breathless and needy, pleading for more. "Harder."

Fuck, it has never felt like this. Pressure builds in my spine, and I know I'm seconds away from release. I clench, fighting off my release, knowing that the longer I hold it, the most explosive it will be.

I pound harder, and Ava cries out. "Oh, my God. That — keep doing that."

Moving my hand from her hip, I bring two fingers to her clit. Applying just enough pressure, I brush the pad of my fingertips across it. She moans, "Yes!"

My whole body tenses up; all I can feel is her squeezing my dick so fucking tight that everything goes blank.

Ava cries out again, her pussy pulsating as she comes all over my cock.

Consumed by euphoric bliss, I thrust once more, following her over the edge.

"Oh, my fuck!"

We both collapse onto the mattress, fully sedated and thoroughly satisfied.

Leaning up on my elbow, I reach over and press my lips against hers.

Pulling back, she hits me with a sleepy, I-just-had-sex smile. "Why —" she releases a heavy breath "— did it take us so long to do that?"

I flop back onto the mattress and cover my forehead with my forearm. "I have no idea. That was —"

"No words," she finishes.

Once I've caught my breath, I roll onto my side and pull her into my chest. "Come here."

I throw my arm over her middle and cup her breast in my hand. "Give me ten minutes, and then we're doing that again."

She chuckles. "Making up for some lost time, are we?"

"Fucking sure we are."

We spend the rest of the night wrapped in a tangle of sweaty limbs, and I know no matter what happens, I am never letting this girl go.

I LAY ON MY BACK, ARMS TUCKED BENEATH MY HEAD, staring up at Ava as she straddles my waist.

Laughter dances in her eyes as she surveys the destruction. "I can't believe you broke my bed."

"I tried to tell you, Avie. IKEA beds are no match for me."

She picks one of her throw pillows off the floor and chucks it at me. "Someone is full of himself."

Lifting my hips, I twist, knocking her off me. Before she has a chance to react, I roll over and cage her beneath me. "Someone will be full of me in a minute if she doesn't stop sassing."

"Oh, Big Man coming in with the threats."

I wiggle my brows, then lean down and mould my lips to hers.

I will never tire of kissing her. Each time her lips meet mine, it sends shivers down my spine.

My phone rings on the bedside locker, and Ava pulls away. I grab hold of her wrist and pull her back against my chest.

"You should probably get that." She props herself up on my chest by resting her hand under her chin. "It's Sunday. Maura won't be happy if you miss two in a row."

Placing a quick kiss on her nose, I reach up from

the floor, grab my phone from the locker and hit the answer button.

"Daniel!" My mother's voice roars through the receiver, almost bursting my eardrum. Suddenly, the phone buzzes with an incoming video call request.

"Why can't I see your face?" She continues.

"Ma! Now isn't a good time to video chat. Can I call you back?"

She blatantly refuses by carrying on the conversation. "I want to show you what I bought for dinner."

Ava bites down on the duvet, concealing her amusement.

Ava knows better than most that all the O'Donoghue boys are Mama's boys. Maura O'Donoghue wouldn't have it any other way.

"I'll be there in an hour. I don't need to see it over the phone. I'm sure whatever you make will be delicious. It always is."

"Are you on the toilet? Is that why you can't spare a moment for your dying mother."

Dying? The woman is barely fifty! I'm pretty sure she is going to outlive the lot of us.

"You're not dying. Stop being so dramatic. And no, I'm not on the toilet. I'm in bed."

Ava's shoulders shake as she tries desperately to

hold in her chuckle. Using my free hand, I poke her side and mouth, "Sshh!"

Somewhere between last night and this morning, Ava decided we need to keep whatever is going on between us a secret, just for a while, knowing that if our mothers found out, they'd be planning our summer wedding before we even figure things out. And although I don't want to hide our relationship — if we can even call it that yet — I get where she is coming from. My mother has been praying for this since I was born, especially when she confirmed I had a penis.

"I can't," she whispers beneath her breath so only I can hear her.

"Who's that?"

"It's nobody, Ma."

Flapping my arms in Ava's direction, I try to silence her laugher with my palm, but the little minx licks me.

"Then why won't you FaceCall me?" Ma insists.

"It's FaceTime, not FaceCall."

I roll my eyes, and a small squeak falls from Avie's mouth.

"Daniel, are you still there?"

"Yeah, still here, but I have to go. I'll be over soon."

"Okay, darling. Oh, before you go, tell Ava I can hear her giggling in the background."

Ava's eyes widen, and my amusement burst past my lips.

It looks as though the cat is out of the bag! I knew we wouldn't get very long before people found out, but fuck me, my mother will tell the whole parish before noon.

"Tell her yourself. I'm bringing her to dinner."

Other People's Expectations

AVA

"Why are you stressing? You've known my mother your whole life. You don't have to impress her. She already loves you."

Looking over my shoulder, I shoot Danny the daggers and ransack my wardrobe for the perfect outfit.

I need help!

What am I supposed to wear to dinner with Maura when her son had his dick parked in my Muff Motel for the night?

Surely you can see how awkward this meal is going to be. "Hey, Maura, lovely roast. And by the way, had I known your son is carrying a spectacular VIP—very impressive penis— I would have listened to you when you urged me to jump on him years ago."

I don't know how to do this, how to act as though we are more than friends but not exclusively dating either.

I know he wants something more, but what does that look like? We haven't exactly had the time to have "*The Conversation*".

Danny steps in behind me and places his hands on my shoulders. Instant calm rushes through my body with just his reassuring touch.

"Take a deep breath, Avie."

I suck in as much air as I can, filling my lungs then slowly exhaling out.

Danny gently turns me to face him and cups my face with his palms. "Talk to me. The only way this is going to work is if we communicate."

My shoulders sag, the tension draining from my body with the weight of his words.

Deciding on honesty is the best policy. I let the words rush from my mouth. "I don't know how to do this. I'm terrified they'll ask questions, and I don't have any answers. "This—" I motion between us "— is so new."

An amused smile curls on his lips, but it does nothing to ease my anxiety.

Grasping his hand in mine, Danny leads me from the bedroom into the living area. He gently pushes my shoulders down until I take a seat on the couch. Once I'm settled, he drops to his hunkers and pulls my hands into his.

"I think it's past time we had a chat about the giant elephant in the room. I'm going to ask you some questions, and I want you to answer them honestly, okay?"

I nod my head, wondering where the hell he's going with this.

"Did last night —" he shoots me a sexy wink, easing some of my worries "— mean anything to you?"

How do I answer that? Of course, it meant something. I wouldn't have risked our friendship over a quick roll in the sack.

Remembering he asked me to be honest, I reply, "Yes."

"Good! Now, would you like a repeat performance? I could probably squeeze another round in before dinner."

I slap his chest, but I can't hold back the smile he put on my face.

"I'm serious. When it comes to you, I'm insatiable."

"Tone it down, Michele Morrone. We're having a grown-up conversation here."

"Who the hell is Michele Morrone?" He chucks.

"Remember that guy from the Netflix porno! Oh, never mind, back to the point, please."

He shakes his head, rolling his eyes in the process. "Ava Marie McCann, you are the only girl I want in my bed at night. You're so ridiculously stubborn, unbelievably sarcastic, and your obsession with the 90s is not healthy. But just like your favourite mythical creature, you're one of a kind. You're my unicorn, Avie, and I wouldn't have it any other way. So, the last question," he pauses, and suddenly all the air in the room dissipates. "Would you like to be my girlfriend?"

"That was the most horrendous proposal for a relationship I have ever heard. You better brush up on that skill for our real proposal, or you'll be finding yourself another wife."

His smile reaches his eyes, highlighting the cheeky dimple in his cheek. "Is that a yes?"

"It's not a no."

SHOULD IT FEEL THIS WEIRD?

I'm heading to Danny's family home as his girlfriend.

Jesus, that's going to take some getting used to.

I dreamt of this day more times than I care to admit, but that doesn't mean that I'm entirely equipped to handle all that comes with that title.

I thought I would have more time to get used to the idea, but there was no going back after Maura called us out this morning.

I could have murdered Danny when he told her I'd be coming for dinner. To say I am ill-prepared is a vast understatement.

Girlfriend, the word tastes foreign on my tongue. Not that I haven't been someone's girlfriend before, but this time it's different. This is Danny.

For so long, I've been the best friend — the crazy girl that says things that I shouldn't say in public. How do we transition?

Surely, you can see my predicament.

"Are you ready for this?" Danny asks as we pull up into his parents' driveway.

"Not by a long shot." I draw in a deep breath, steadying my rambling thoughts and calming the bundle of nerves that are bouncing around my stomach.

Danny rounds the front of his Ford Ranger, opening my door, and I hop down.

It's okay, Ava. It's not as though you haven't met these people before.

You grew up in this house.

It's just dinner.

"Stop worrying," he leans forward, placing a kiss on my forehead.

"There is a lot to think about, Danny. Our new relationship doesn't only affect us. I'm friends with your brothers. Your mam is a crucial part of my life. I don't know if I'm ready for the pressure they'll undoubtedly place on us. Even if they don't mean to."

Gripping my hips, he pulls me closer, soothing me with his I-give-no-fucks smile.

"Avie, what goes on between us has nothing to do with anyone else. We decide on how we want this to go."

"I know, it all seems a little fast, though. It's so new, D. I just don't want to rush into this because of other people's expectations."

Lifting his hand to my face, he brushes my hair behind my ear with his fingertips. "We aren't rushing.

This thing between us has been brewing for years. I get that you are scared. I am too. But trust me when I say I'd never do anything that would make me lose you. We've got this."

"We've got this," I repeat, feeling somewhat calmer.

"On three?"

"Three."

Together we walk hand in hand, ready to face everyone for the first time as a couple.

But my new-found confidence wears off rather quickly. Especially when we walk into Danny's childhood living room and his entire family stands, clapping as if we just safely landed an aeroplane that was missing its engine.

Is it too late to run?

OKAY, SO STANDING OVATION ASIDE, THIS HASN'T BEEN too bad.

Maura has only hinted at her non-existent grandbabies once. As for Danny's brothers, they've been pretty chill — even stating that Danny and I have been practically dating for years, without the benefit of pre-marital sex.

They're not wrong.

For once, I almost feel sorry for the ghosts of our exes past — Moany Mandy included.

Honestly, they never stood a chance because even though Danny and I weren't physically involved, on an emotional level, we were.

Today opened my eyes. It must have been difficult for the people we dated to accept my and Danny's friendship. We've always been in sync. I put it down to the strength of our friendship, but I realise now, it's more than that.

Sure, the transition from friends to lovers won't be easy. And lord knows, it will be weird for a while, but I love weird. I believe that if we stay open and honest, just like Danny suggested, we can work this out together.

Danny's hand finds mine underneath Maura's dining room table. He leans left, bringing his face closer to mine, and whispers for only me to hear. "Are you doing okay?"

His hand squeezes mine, a small gesture of reassurance.

I flash him a genuine smile. "I'm great."

He winks, his smile mirroring mine. "Me too, babe."

Four letters, and my heart goes into cardiac arrest.

My shock must be written on my face because the bastard smiles wider and raises his brows. "Babe, babe, babe!"

I swat his harder-than-stone pecs. "Shut up, idiot."

"So, Ava," Maura pulls my attention away from her son. "Your mam was telling me you're trying to open a salon soon. How's that going?" She passes the bowl of mashed potatoes to Keegan and waits for my reply with a smile on her face.

Lifting my fork off the table, I nervously shift the peas around my plate. "Emm, yeah. Charlie and I are in the process of getting a loan. We have our final meeting the morning after Danny's big fight. So all going well, we should be up and running before Christmas."

"That's great. I'm proud of you, honey. You girls are far too good at what you do to be working for someone else."

"Do you have a premises' in mind?" Peter inquires.

"Yeah, we've been looking at the old bakery across from the gym. It's been neglected for so long, and the location is perfect."

"It's a great spot," Peter adds. "Well, if you need a hand fixing the place up, I could spare a few strapping young men," he hints at his three sons. "Isn't that right, boys?"

Keegan, Kye, and Danny erupt into a chorus of yeah's.

I don't know why I was so worried about today. Maura and Peter have always treated me like one of their own. I should have known that dating Danny wouldn't change that.

They're good people, and I love them dearly.

Maybe this will be easier than I thought.

Netflix And Chill

AVA

I HAVE HAD ENOUGH OF THIS DAY. MY FEET ARE aching; my jeans are too tight, and I'm so hungry I could eat the three-day-old soup that's in the staff room fridge.

Thankfully, I only have one client left. Then I can go home, put on my pyjamas, and veg out on the couch with my boyfriend. Ugh, even after two weeks, that still rolls off the tongue with a touch of awkwardness.

Our new development has taken some getting used

to. For instance, I can now touch him whenever the need strikes. Oh, and no more averting my eyes when he strolls into the room half-naked, in just a towel.

There's also the fact that we live together, so when I'm tired with all the touchy-feely, I can't get rid of him. Okay, so that last one hasn't been a problem. If anything, we've both been too busy to spend any time together.

With Danny's fight coming up this weekend, he's been spending all his time at the gym.

Hence, the reason I'm so eager to hightail it out of here. Danny promised me a date night, and I'm hoping he knows me well enough to know that a date night includes Netflix, pizza, and beer. Not some anxiety-inducing socials and uncomfortable seats at a movie theatre.

Suddenly, the salon door swings open, knocking off the tiny bell hanging over the door. Lifting my head from the reception computer, I come face to face with my favourite client.

"Well, if it isn't Lily Maguire." I round the desk and greet her with a genuine smile.

Lily has been a client of mine for years, and I take pride in knowing I am the artist behind her famous vibrant red tresses.

"Hey, Ava. I hope you're ready to tame this mane."

"Would you stop! You look as radiant as you always do," I compliment.

"Says you. Every time I see you, I die of hair envy." She removes her leather jacket, shakes off the raindrops, then hangs it on the coat rack beside the door.

"Where do you want me?"

"Follow me."

Once I get her seated in my section, I run my fingers through her hair. "So, what are you thinking, just a root touch-up or something different?"

She pulls her phone out of her designer bag and clicks open her Pinterest app. Lifting it over her shoulder, she shows me an image of a girl with bright red roots that bleed into orange tips.

"I love this. It screams boss bitch who takes no prisoners."

Gazing down at the phone, I nod in approval. "Yes, I love the flame effect, and it would look amazing on you. Give me two minutes, and I will whip up the colours."

"Perfect."

As much as I loved catching up with Lily and all the news from the latest 4Clover tour, I am glad I'm finally home.

I open the front door, hoping to find Danny, but instead, darkness greets me.

He must have got held up at the gym. It looks like I'll be ordering dinner for one.

After flicking on the side lamp, I toss my keys in the bowl and pull off my boots.

Nothing in this world compares to the feeling of removing your shoes after a long day — heavenly bliss.

I pad down the small hallway to the living room and come to a standstill.

What in the romance novel is this?

My round eyes scan every inch of the room.

Bedsheets are hanging from the ceiling, making my tiny living room look like a fort. Fairy lights light up the darkened space, giving off a soft and romantic glow. The floor is littered with blankets and throw pillows, creating a giant bed in the middle of the room. The mantle above the electric fire holds my favourite Yankee candle — Midnight Jasmine — and the scent of water jasmine, sweet honeysuckle, and mandarin blossom fill the room. And last, but by no means least, is my best friend — I mean boyfriend —

is standing in the midst of it all, holding up a six-pack of beers and a large sixteen-inch pizza box, wearing nothing but a pair of grey lounge pants.

Have I died? Is this what heaven looks like?

If I didn't already love this man, this would be the pivotal moment where my heart would jump right into his hands.

"Happy first official date."

Could someone pass me a dictionary because I have no words!

"Say something," he prompts.

"I love you. I mean, I love it, this. The fort." *Oh, my shit! I was not supposed to say that.*

Danny places the beers and pizza on the coffee table and stalks towards me like a predator seeking his prey. The distance between us closes, and I lose my breath when I see the hungry look in his eyes.

His hands cup my cheeks, and suddenly his lips are on mine, sweeping me up in a kiss that would burn down cities.

Finally, after leaving me breathless, he pulls back. His deep brown eyes home in on mine. "Say it again," he whispers.

A whirlwind of nervous energy ripples through my chest, but somehow, he eases my fear of rejection with the undeniable love shining from his smile.

Swallowing back the giant lump lodged in my throat, I cover his hands with mine. "I love you."

In one swift motion, Danny lifts me off my feet. My legs instantly lock around his waist, and he carries me over to the makeshift bed. He lays me down gently and covers my body with his. My hand glides over his half sleeve of tattoos, up to his triceps, stopping at his shoulders.

Our eyes lock, and an indescribable feeling lingers in the silence between us. Anticipation floods the room, years of pent-up emotions sweeping us up in a tidal wave and drawing us away from the safety of the shore.

"I love you, too, Avie."

This is it. There is no going back. We jumped, and now we have to pray we can survive the fall. When a person can talk to you without speaking, love you without touching, and fill your world with colour with just a smile — that is when you know you have found the person destined for you.

Sometimes they're family.

Sometimes they're friends.

Sometimes they're lovers.

And if you're lucky, they'll be all three.

We collide with a kiss that leads to roaming

hands. Item by item, Danny pulls our clothes off, leaving us skin to skin beneath the fairy light glow.

Suddenly, Danny is towering above me with lust-filled eyes.

He pushes inside me, and the world fades away. It's just him and me.

His movements are slow, sweet, and tender. Each thrust reaches a place that physically can't be touched. His hands caress my skin, soft and gentle, painting his love onto my soul.

His lips skate across my neck, teasing me with his hot breaths and torturous nibbles.

A needy moan breaks past my lips, begging him for everything he is willing to give.

This is not like any other time. The feeling of something more becomes too prominent to ignore.

He grips my wrists, gradually bringing them above my head as he continues to rock into me. His eyes are wild as he grinds against me. My back arches off the floor, chasing the high and embracing the fall.

"Ava." He cherishes each letter as it rolls off his tongue, wrapped up in ecstasy.

His grip on my wrists tightens as he deepens his thrusts, soothing the ache between my thighs.

The tingling starts in my stomach, gaining momentum and spreading to every nerve ending.

Clenching my muscles, I squeeze him tight. My legs shake, quivering as my orgasm reaches its climax. Lightning courses through my body, and I submerge myself in it.

The intensity of his gaze holds me hostage; I am lost to him, in him, for him.

He grinds into me once more, finally succumbing to his release.

"No more what if's, Avie. It's you. It will always be you."

His grip on my wrists loosens, and my hands move to his face. I cup his cheeks, drawing him in and brushing my lips against his.

We spend the rest of the night underneath the bright glow of fairy lights, my head on his chest and his hand tangled in my hair. We drink warm beer, eat cold pizza, and binge-watch our favourite shows.

Some women prefer fine dining and flowers, but I'm more than happy, naked in the arms of my best friend, enjoying some good ole fashioned, Netflix and chill.

Show Up Or Step Out

AVA

"Hey, Cee-Cee," Kye greets as I push through the large, double glass doors of Game On Fitness with my hands full of bags. "Did you come to see your boy in action?"

"Sure did, and I brought carbs," I wiggle my brows, making him laugh.

He catapults across the reception desk, pulls one of the bags from my hands and lifts it to his nose. "Fuck, that smells like heaven. What is that?"

"It's Keegan's famous spaghetti bolognese. There's enough in there to feed an army."

A deep groan rumbles from his mouth. "If you ever get tired of dating my brother, just know that I would happily take his place."

"Hey." Danny's deep brogue comes from behind me. "Keep your paws away from my girlfriend," He reprimands Kye.

Turning on my heel, I come face to chest with Danny's sweat covered pecs.

My eyes scan his larger-than-life frame, noting every dip, ridge, and crevice, finally coming to a halt at the emerald-green waistband of his Vale Tudo compression shorts.

I force my gaze back to the angular lines of his face, and my eyes lock on his. Something dark and dangerous lingers in their depths, and I'd be lying if I said it doesn't turn me on.

"Like what you see, Avie?" His tone is light and teasing as he flashes me a naughty smile.

I run my tongue along the roof of my mouth and swallow the lump of desire residing in my throat.

Deciding to tease him, I quip, "I've seen better." He knows damn well what his body does to mine, but there is no need for me to announce it to the entire gym.

He steps into my space, and without removing his

eyes from mine, he takes the bags from my hands and gives them to Kye.

Suddenly, he pulls me against his chest then lifts my chin with his wrapped hand. "You look gorgeous."

I look down at my gym outfit — pastel pink Nike shorts and a matching top that's unzipped, revealing my mint green sports bra. "I came prepared in case you needed a sparring partner."

Tomorrow's fight is important to Danny, and rightly so. It has the potential to pave the way for a life-changing UFC career. He has worked his ass off to get to this point. And I will do whatever I can to help him achieve that dream — even if that means spending my day off in a sweaty gym.

"All you need to do is show up, right?"

His lips curl up at my Conor McGregor reference.

Suddenly, he presses his mouth against mine in an earth-shattering kiss that makes my knees weak.

"Excuse me!" Kye interrupts. "This is a public place. Can we keep the PDA to a minimum?"

"You're just jealous," Danny laughs, throwing his arm around my shoulder.

"Damn right, I am."

We follow Kye into the staff room, and he pulls out some plates.

"So," I prompt while serving "how's the training going?"

"Good. We ran five miles before breakfast, then we came back here and hit the bags."

I pass them a full plate each, and they dig in.

"Do you think your knee will hold up?" I'm showing my concern, but I can't help it. Every time Danny steps into that octagon, he's at risk, and although I love and support his career, it doesn't ease the anxiety I feel every time he fights.

"Yeah, he should be good to go," Kye answers between mouthfuls. "He just needs to make sure he keeps his guard up. One bad blow, and it is game over."

"Less of the negativity," Danny shuts him down. "I'll be fine. I'm at the peak of my career. Rian Collins may be the newest UFC prodigy, but this is my time. I feel it in my bones."

Leaning across, I kiss his cheek. "I don't doubt it."

IT'S SAFE TO SAY I WILL NEVER TIRE OF WATCHING Danny in his element. When he steps into that octagon, gone is the fun-loving teddy bear I know and love, replaced by an unstoppable, wild beast of a man who radiates strength and power.

"That boy is something special," Danny's dad admires from the stool beside me. "I've been at this game for thirty-eight years, and never have I seen anyone fight with the passion that he does."

My gaze moves back to Danny, and I watch with curious fascination as he bounces around the canvas on the balls off his feet.

"He is certainly a sight."

Beads of sweat kiss the surface of Danny's skin, trickling down his taut muscles as he jabs right and left, preparing for his sparring match against Kye.

"Does it ever get easier?" I ask Peter. "Watching them step into the cage, knowing that eventually, they will get hurt."

"Nah, that feeling never fades, especially when you love the person more than life itself. Back in my fighting days, Maura would be a bag of nerves before every fight, but she always showed up. And that's what it's about, Ava — showing up, and making sure your person knows that you'll be in their corner, no matter what."

Kye steps into the cage. "Hope you're ready for me to kick your ass in front of your girlfriend, brother."

Danny throws his head back, laughing at Kye as he bounces around like a chimpanzee. "Not going to happen. I could beat you blindfolded, and you know it."

My body shudders, knowing that in a few seconds, fists will be flying.

"You know," Peter drags my attention back to him. "Danny adores you. He always has. But fighting is in his blood, Ava. He can't, not step into that ring — it's who he is. If you love him like I think you do, you'll find a way to ease the ache you feel when he steps onto that canvas. Five minutes, three rounds, one second at a time."

I nod in understanding, knowing that to love Danny, I have to be okay with his career.

"So, what will it be," he prods. "Show up or step out?"

I think back to earlier when I joked with Danny in the reception area.

All you gotta do is show up.

I turn my attention back to the octagon and clap my hands together. "Right, ladies, enough hanging around. Let's get this show on the road."

"Oh, the lady wants to see what Danny the Dominator's got!" Kye shouts as he lunges for Danny, striking out with a quick left cross.

Danny dodges right, kicking out with his left leg and catching Kye in the ribs.

I hold my breath as Kye stumbles. Danny takes the opportunity to strike hard and fast. He rushes forward, lifting Kye off his feet, then slams him onto the floor.

My heart pounds as they grapple. Suddenly, Danny locks Kye in a leg tangle, immobilising him. His elbow wraps around Kye's left arm, and he pulls, causing Kye to tap out.

Danny's eyes flash to mine. "How was that, babe?" He winks with a broad smile and lust dancing around his eyes.

Before I can reply, Kye's foot slides out, sweeping Danny off his feet.

He hits the canvas with a loud thump, and I can't help the laughter that rumbles from my chest.

"And that, lady and gent, is how you catch your opponent off guard." Kye stands and takes a bow.

Danny sits up, hugging his knees with his arms.

Peter stands from his stool and rubs his palms off his thighs. "I'm heading off before your mother comes looking for me. Make sure you boys lock up before you leave. And don't overdo it. Tomorrow is a new day. You'll need all the energy you've got to take down Rian Collins this weekend. He's fast, even if that left hook will send him spinning."

"We won't," Kye assures Peter as he holds out his hand and helps Danny off the floor. "One more round, and we will turn in for the night."

"Good. See you tomorrow, Ava."

"Night, Peter."

When Peter leaves, Kye climbs out of the ring and picks me up off the stool. "Your turn, Cee-Cee. Bring him to his knees."

Kye drops me into the ring with a chuckle. "Show him how it's done, Cee-Cee."

A devious look flashes in Danny's eyes, and he lifts his hand, flapping his fingers in a come-to-me gesture.

I have no idea what I am doing — other than the few moves Danny taught me in his self-defence classes — but I'll give it my best shot.

Channelling my inner Mr Miyagi, I decide defence is the best offence and wait for Danny to attack.

He stalks towards me, and two in seconds flat, he lifts me off my feet and slams me into the floor. *Okay, so he didn't slam me, gently placed might be more accurate.*

He holds himself above me with a wicked smile, relishing in my defeat.

I knew I should have gone with the Cobra Kai mantra.

Strike first. Strike hard. No Mercy.

Stay Focused, D

DANNY

Cameras flash as I stand with my team in the backstage tunnels of the 3arena. My tri-coloured robe hangs heavy on my shoulders, reminding me of the importance of tonight's event.

This is it — the most crucial moment of my fighting career.

If I win tonight, I am guaranteed a ticket to the UFC fight night in Vegas next spring.

"One minute until we walk." The woman in charge of entrances announces.

I bounce on the balls of my feet, releasing the

pent-up energy that is coursing through my veins. Rolling my shoulders, I shake out my arms.

"Show me your hands," Kye lifts my fists, scanning my wraps, making sure they're secure.

"Thirty seconds."

"Remember to stay off the knee. Keep your guard up, and focus. Rian is fast, so stay moving, then when you see an opening, hit him with a left. If that doesn't work —"

"— take him to the canvas." Knowing what I need to do, I cut Kye off.

"Five."

The countdown begins.

"Four."

I crack my neck, moving my head from side to side.

"Three."

"You got this." Kye's hands land on my shoulder, encouraging me with just a look.

"Two."

"It's my time."

"One."

"It's your time."

"Walk."

The opening bars of *'Till I Collapse* by Eminem

blares through the surround sound, and that's my cue to get moving.

I shift on my feet, throwing jab after jab as we make our way through the tunnels and into the awaiting crowd.

The security parts the sea of people, clearing a path for my team and me. As I enter the arena, the crowd roars wildly, filling my body with adrenaline.

I'm ready. I feel it in my bones.

We reach the octagon, and I spot my ma, da, Keegan, and Ava standing ringside, right behind my corner.

Pulling away from my team, I head in their direction.

"Danny!" Kye shouts. "Where the fuck are you going? It's showtime."

Ignoring him, I head for my girl.

I reach her in four strides, wrap my arms around her waist, and lift her off her feet.

My lips meet Ava's, and the crowd roars louder. I pull back and stare into her eyes.

As much as Ava has tried to hide it, I know she's nervous about tonight, but in true Ava fashion, she shows up anyway, cheering me on like she always does.

"I love you."

She takes my face between her palms. "I love you, too. Now, go! And for the love of my sanity, don't get hurt."

Her lips press against mine, soft, sweet and far too fucking fleeting.

Walking backwards, I keep my eyes on the love of my life. "I love you." I mouth before climbing into the cage.

"LADIES AND GENTLEMEN, THIS FIGHT IS THREE rounds in the European featherweight division. Introducing first, fighting out of the blue corner, a mixed martial artist holding a semi-professional record of eight wins and two losses. He stands six-feet-five-inches tall, weighing in at one-hundred-and-forty-five-pounds, fighting out of Dublin, Ireland. Danny the Dominator O'Donoghue."

I bounce around the ring, swinging my fists from left to right, keeping my muscles loose.

Adrenaline pumps through my veins as I stare down my opponent. The rowdy crowd roar, singing out Irish anthems at the top of their lungs.

I got this. Dublin is my hometown; this is my crowd, my fight.

"And now, introducing his opponent," The announcer continues, his booming voice igniting a fire amongst the crowd. "Fighting out of the red corner. This man is a mixed martial artist, holding a professional record of eighteen wins and six losses. He stands at six-feet-two inches, weighing in at one-hundred-and-forty-six-pounds, fighting out of Glasgow, Scotland. Rian the Raven Collins.

Taking one last look at Ava, I shoot her a wink.

She lifts her hand to her painted bright pink mouth and blows me a kiss.

The referee calls us to the centre, and I square my shoulders and pop my game face on.

Hands up, the ref calls, "Fight." and Rian rushes forward as predicted. He swings right, and his fist connects with my ribs.

I step back, keeping my guard up, hoping he tires himself out.

He comes at me again, this time from the left. I lift my right leg, blocking him, and connecting my knee with his chest in the process. He gasps, drawing in a breath after I winded him.

Kye was right, this guy is fast, but his precision could use some work.

Kye's voice soars above the crowd. "Stay focused, D. Keep the guard up, and shoot for the right."

Rian hears Kye's instructions, and he does precisely what Kye hoped. He lifts his right arm, leaving his left side wide open. With brute force, I swing hard and fast, connecting with his jaw. His head pivots right. He's dazed, but unfortunately, still standing.

Finally, the round comes to a close, and I head for my corner. Dropping onto my stool, Kye climbs into the cage and sprays water in my mouth.

"You're doing great," he encourages. "How's the knee?"

Gargling the water, I turn my head, and I spit into the bucket. "It's holding up."

"Good. Just watch those leg kicks. If one of those connects, you'll buckle."

I nod, trying to keep my head in the game.

Two more rounds.

AVA

We're in the final round, and it's tied at one to one. My stomach is seconds away from expelling its contents all over the arena floor — dramatic, I think not.

Never, and I do mean, never, have I ever felt this

kind of anxiety. My nerves are so shot, I'm surprised I have any fingernails left.

I shift in my seat, trying to stop my leg from digging a hole in the floor.

Maura's hand lands on my thigh. "Almost there, sweetheart. Deep breaths."

Keeping my eyes on Danny, I acknowledge her with a nod of my head, unable to form words. I shift forward, hanging on the edge of my seat.

A river of red flows from Danny's left brow, making my urge to climb up into that octagon and shove my high heeled foot up Rian Collins' ass grows stronger.

This is excruciating. Watching the man I love go pound for pound is not all it's cracked up to be. I am sweating in places I didn't know I could sweat, and my stomach has taken up permanent residence in my throat, and yet, I can't look away. I need to know he is okay.

Grappling on the canvas, Rian cages Danny beneath him. Lifting my hands, I cup my lips and shout, "Come on, D. Get up."

Danny twists his legs around Rian's torso and shifts his hips, freeing himself from Rian's hold.

"On your feet, son," Peter shouts. He knows better than anyone that Danny needs to keep off the mat. In the second round, Rian showed off his excellent grappling skills. Danny needs to keep him moving.

"Forty seconds," Maura counts.

Danny hops up and bounces from side to side. Swinging forward with a right hook, he connects with Rian's rib cage.

"That's it, D!"

Rian slaps out, connecting with Danny's cheek. Then it happens, Rian kicks forward, connecting with Danny's bad knee.

The crowd fades to nothing when a horrendous pop floods the air. Time slows as Danny's leg buckles out from beneath him. His agony is written all over his face as he falls forward, hitting the canvas.

I jump out of my seat, rushing over to the edge of the cage. Peter grips my shoulder, keeping me from climbing inside. "You can't go in there, Ava."

Kye launches over the cage walls and rushes to Danny's side as I stand there feeling utterly helpless while the love of my life lies unmoving on the octagon floor.

The noise of the crowd dulls, and all I hear is an unbearable ringing in my ears.

Keegan wraps his arms around me, pulling me

into his chest. "He'll be okay, Cee-Cee," he tries his best to reassure me, but his attempt is futile.

Peeling away from Keegan's embrace, I watch in horror as the on-site medical team straps Danny to a gurney and carts him out of the cage.

One Strike, And Game Over

DANNY

"I'M SORRY TO SAY IT'S BAD NEWS."

The doctor's words echo in my ear.

"Complete tear."

"Anterior Cruciate Ligament."

"Surgery."

"Fuck." Kye mutters, reminding me that my entire family is here to witness my downfall.

I shake my head, unwilling to hear anymore.

I am done.

Everything I've worked so hard for, all my dreams, gone in a split second.

One strike, and game over.

One wrongly placed kick, and I hit the ground like a ton of bricks.

Ava's soft, gentle voice breaks through the white noise.

"Will he fight again?"

I squeeze my eyes shut, and grind down on my teeth, bracing myself for the doctor's following words.

"I'm afraid it's too soon to tell. We will need to reassess that when the time comes. For now, Danny needs to focus on easing the swelling. Then in a few weeks, we can perform the ACL reconstruction."

"So, it's not off the cards?" Kye questions. "He may be able to get in the cage again."

"I can't say for definite. All going well, recovery time is estimated anywhere between six and twelve months, with rehabilitation."

The doctor releases a heavy sigh, seeming frustrated by their constant questioning.

I know the feeling, mate.

Even if I recover within the year, and that's a big fucking if, I've still missed my shot.

I'm almost thirty. I can't afford to lose another year — my time is running out.

"When will the surgery take place?" My mother queries. Her voice is dripping with concern.

"We would hope the knee would be ready within the next six to eight weeks."

"When can I leave?" It's the first question to leave my mouth. But it's the only one I want answers to. I've had enough of this place, the worry radiating from my family, and the sympathetic look in Ava's eyes. I need to get out of here, away from it all.

"You can go home tonight once I run through the pre-ACL surgery regime."

Turning to face me, the doctor politely asks everyone to wait outside.

"Kye can stay," I pipe up. "He's my personal trainer. He'll be working with me throughout my recovery."

The doctor nods, and Kye takes a seat while everyone else shuffles out of the room.

Ava hangs back, kissing my forehead. "I'll be outside. If you need me, just shout."

I nod, avoiding her eyes.

Looking at her, the other half of my dream hurts too much. How can I give her the life she deserves when all I've ever known has gone up in flames? She deserves better, not some banged up fighter with no career prospects.

She senses my frustration, but she knows me well

enough not to push. "Well, I'll just... emm." She backs out the door with a half-broken smile.

"What's the plan, Doc?" Kye prompts.

Turning to face me, the doctor lists off my treatment plan. "Initially, the knee needs to be protected. I'd like for you to keep it secure with a knee mobiliser. We'll start with two crutches to avoid full weight-bearing, then in a week or so, you can move to just one. Controlling the swelling is the main priority, so apply ice regularly, and keep the leg elevated as much as you can."

"Okay, and what about exercise?"

"Once the swelling and pain ease, you can do some light walking, no stairs. Then in about three weeks, you can bring in some closed-chained exercises to help regain motion — for example, leg presses, toe-ups, hamstring curls, and wall-side squats. Be mindful not to overexert. Keep the sessions short and build it up."

Kye makes some notes, but I zone out, letting the anger boiling under my skin take over.

Once the doctor leaves to get my release forms, I shuffle to the edge of the bed and attempt to swing my legs over the edge.

Kye jumps from his chair and helps me sit up.

If there's anyone who completely understands the

turmoil I'm in, it's him. This time two years ago, he was right where I am, laying in this hospital, receiving the news that his fighting career had just gone down the shitter.

He knows what it's like to have your lifelong dream ripped from your grasp. Sure, I could bounce back, but everyone knows that my knee will never be the same again — trying to pretend otherwise is a waste of fucking time.

Kye understands that. He's been in this bed. He's worn the shoes my feet are in.

I don't want Ava's sympathy. I don't want my mother's coddling. I don't want my dad and Keegan's encouragements.

"Tell me what you need," Kye prompts.

I need to be left alone.

"Can I stay with you?"

Judging from the look in his eyes, he doesn't like it, but he doesn't push. "Sure."

My hospital room door swings open, and Ava steps inside. "Hey, the doctor said you're free to go. Do you want me to get the car?"

I hate the way she's looking at me — sad, pitiful eyes and a wistful smile.

Turning my head towards Kye, I nod for him to give us a minute.

Using his arms, he pushes himself out of the chair.

The door closes behind him, and Ava rounds the bed to face me. "Is everything okay?"

No, Avie. Nothing is okay.

I don't say that, though. "The doctor said I need to avoid stairs, so I'm going to go stay with Kye for a while."

She reaches forward, taking hold of my hand. "Okay. I suppose that makes the most sense. I can swing by the apartment and get you some stuff and drop it off."

I run my thumb across her knuckles. "That would be great, thanks."

"It's no trouble."

She leans forward, pressing her lips against mine in a tender kiss. I pull back, and her eyebrows narrow, forming a v between her eyes.

She steps back, clearly hurt by my rejection, but I just can't deal with the lovey shit right now.

My world, as I know it, has fallen apart. I don't know who I am outside of the octagon. Sue me if I need to take a minute to figure it out.

AVA

As I haul Danny's bag up Kye's driveway, an unsettling feeling unravels in my stomach.

I can't even imagine how Danny must be feeling after having his dreams thrown up in the air and praying like fuck, they'll have a soft, safe landing.

The image of him sitting on that hospital bed will haunt me for the rest of my life. He looked so lost, so broken, and there wasn't a goddamn thing I could do to help ease his pain.

I won't lie — the vacant look in his once bright eyes scared me shitless. It's awful to watch someone you love close down and push the world out, especially when you have no idea how to make them hang on.

Danny is too stubborn to lean on anyone, always thinking he needs to be the big strong man. I need to show him that I'm here. No matter how challenging the road may be, we will get through this together.

It's all about showing up and letting him know you're in his corner.

Peter's words stick out in my mind, reassuring me that everything will be okay.

Sometimes we have to deal with shitty stuff. Life is never an easy ride.

There will be good days filled with laughter.

Bad days filled with doubt.

Then there will be days like today, where we need to pull up our big girl socks and be there for the ones we love.

I reach the front door, and Kye answers, motioning for me to come in. "Hey Cee-Cee," he pulls me into a brotherly hug. "How are you holding up?"

"I'm okay. How's Danny doing?"

Kye's gaze drops to the floor. "Not gonna lie, he's not in a good place."

Shrugging my shoulders, I release a heavy sigh. "I suppose that's to be expected."

"He'll come around." He assures me. "Do you want to check on him?"

I nod my head.

"He's in the spare room. The second door on the left."

Coming to a stop outside the door, I draw in a much-needed breath, then raise my hand and rap my knuckles against the solid wood. "D, it's Ava. Can I come in?"

His reply is short and clipped. "Yes."

My fingers grip the handle, and I press down and push the door open.

Danny lays on his back, staring up at the ceiling. "Hey, I brought you some things. Where do you want me to leave them?"

"Thanks. You can just throw it there. I'll go through it in the morning."

Gently, I place the bag on the floor.

"Is there anything I can do for you? Can I get you something to eat or drink?"

"I'm fine," he grunts.

I sit on the edge of the bed and reach for his hand. "Are you sure?"

"I said I'm fine," he barks.

I hate knowing that he's suffering. On an average day, I would call him out for his bullshit, but I know he's caught up over everything, so I let it slide.

"It's going to be okay, D. I promise. With the ACL reconstruction, you'll be back on your feet in no time. You can recover from this."

His head whips in my direction, and the look that's brewing behind those chocolate brown eyes slices my chest wide open.

"Nothing about this situation is okay. Even if I regain full strength in my knee, I'm done, Ava. I'm almost thirty. This was my last chance, and now, it's over. So, please, don't fucking sit there and tell me it's going to be okay. When I know fucking well, it won't be."

"Danny—"

"Just leave, Ava. I have enough on my plate without you being here making promises you can't keep."

"Don't do this. Don't shut me out."

"GO!" His roar is so loud. It rattles my bones.

Standing from the bed, I decide to give him some space.

"Fine! If that's what you want."

I stop in the doorway and peer over my shoulder. Making one last attempt to reach him, I let Danny know I'm here if he needs me. "I love you, Danny."

His eyes stay focused on the ceiling, ignoring me as I walk away.

When I reach the living room, Kye stands and wraps his arms around me. "Give him some time, Cee-Cee. He's mad at the world right now. He'll come around."

I know Kye is right, but his words don't ease the ache in my chest or stop the tears welling in my eyes.

It Ain't Over Until The Final Bell Rings

AVA

AFTER SPENDING THE ENTIRE NIGHT TOSSING, turning, and reliving the nightmare that was yesterday, I eventually drag my exhausted body from Danny's bed and head for a hot shower.

Charlie and I have our meeting with the bank this afternoon, and although I'm the furthest thing possible away from, *in the mood* — I can't let this opportunity slip by.

Charlie and I have worked long and hard to get to this point, and it wouldn't be fair to her — or me —

if I let my personal life get in the way of what we've spent years trying to achieve.

As I stand under the hot spray of the shower, my mind drifts to Danny. I have never seen him lash out the way he did last night — it's just not who he is.

His usual happy-go-lucky demeanour was gone, buried underneath the rubble of what he thinks he's lost.

My mind is a maze of thoughts, swirling so fast I can't grasp them.

Logically, I know I need to give him some space and let him process everything, but the emotional side of me wants to rush to his side, wrap him up in my arms, and tell him it's going to be okay.

I have no idea how to handle this.

It's not as though I can throw out some highly inappropriate comment and hope for the best. I need to be a grown-up, and unfortunately, that doesn't come naturally for me.

Once I feel semi-alive, I hop out of the shower and busy myself with getting ready for my meeting. When I finish blow-drying my hair and applying a light coverage of foundation, I pull on my pale pink, tailored cigarette pants and white blouse. Looking somewhat respectable, I pop on my rose gold stilettos and head out the door, resisting the urge to call Danny and check-in.

Kye was right, he needs space to gather his thoughts, and he can't do that if I'm hovering over him.

Kye has been there, so if anyone knows what Danny is feeling right now, it's him.

I just hope to God that Kye can pull him out of his misery before Danny gets lost down a very dark rabbit hole.

I spend the drive to Charlie's, lost in thought, and when I pull into her driveway, I don't even remember how I got here.

"Hey," Charlie greets me with a rueful smile as she hops into the passenger seat. "How's Danny? Any word?"

I shake my head from left to right. "No. He hasn't called. I'm trying to give him some space. But not knowing if he's okay is killing me."

Lifting her hand, she places it on my forearm. "I'm sure he'll call soon, Ava."

I swallow back my sadness and change the subject. I need to think about anything else, anything but Danny. "How's Tadhg?"

She flops back into her seat and rolls her eyes.

The last time we spoke, she said they've been

having problems, but I've been so consumed with all things Danny that I haven't had the time to really chat with her.

"He is not on board with this salon idea. He wants me to be barefoot and pregnant, not opening a business. It's just so frustrating. Don't get me wrong, I want kids, eventually. But right now, I want to do something for me."

Tilting her head towards me, she releases a heavy breath. "Does that make me selfish?"

Taking my eyes off the road for a split second, I turn my head to face her. "No. It doesn't. It's not the nineteen-sixties, anymore."

Averting my gaze back on the road, I add. "If Tadhg can't get on board with your dreams, put him in the bin. Nobody needs that negativity in their life. You deserve better."

"If only life were that simple," she sighs.

"Tell me about it."

LOAN APPROVED.

Those two words have played in my mind repeatedly since Charlie and I left the bank this afternoon.

I should be on top of the world, but somehow, all I feel is guilt.

How is it fair that I've become closer to my dream in the space of twenty-four hours while Danny has just had his ripped away?

I should be elated, dancing on the rooftops and singing from the tips of my lungs, but instead, all I feel is dread.

How am I supposed to tell Danny that everything I have worked towards has finally come to fruition? I can't, not when he's dealing with a torn ACL and a career that seems so far out of his reach?

I know he couldn't be with me today. But there is still a tiny part of me that is annoyed he didn't bother to text. I know he has a lot going on, but the thought would have been nice. It's a big day for me.

"It's okay." Charlie hands me a cup of tea as she plops herself down on the couch beside me.

"What?"

"It's okay to be happy." Charlie wraps her arm around my shoulder and pulls me against her chest. "I know you're feeling bad because of everything that Danny is going through. But you need to stop feeling guilty."

"I know, but I can't help it. It doesn't seem fair."

Her hand caresses my hair. "It's not. But that's

life, Ava. Shitty things happen to good people, but the world still has to turn no matter what happens. You can't pause your happiness because your boyfriend is having a rough time. And knowing Danny, he wouldn't want you to, either."

My head knows she's right, but my heart sings a different tune.

DANNY

"Leg up," Kye lifts my leg onto the coffee table and props it up with one of his throw pillows. "How'd you sleep?"

Wiggling around on his couch, I try to get comfortable. "Like shit."

"Are the pain meds not helping?"

I wish I could say my knee was the reason I tossed and turned all night, but it wasn't.

It had a hell of a lot more to do with the aggressive way I spoke to Avie.

Guilt gnaws at me, eating away at my insides.

Sure, I have every right to be pissed while I'm stuck in this limbo of what the fuck do I do now. But that certainly does not give me the right to roar at her the way I did. I wouldn't blame her if she told me to go fuck myself.

"They're fine."

He plops himself into the recliner facing me. "Danny, I know you have a lot on your plate. Trust me, I get it. But pushing everyone out is not going to fix what happened."

"I know that, Kye. I just can't have people falling all over me trying to make it right. I need to be realistic. There is a very big chance that I may never step foot in the cage again. And having Ava, or Ma, or even Keegan telling me that I can get through this is not what I want to hear right now."

"I get it."

"Does it get any easier?"

"Honestly? Not really. Don't get me wrong, I love what I do, but every day I miss it. The adrenaline of the fight, the roar of the crowd, the high I felt when I won. I miss it all. But Danny, just because it didn't end well for me doesn't mean you'll be handed the same fate."

I bow my head. "I know that. But I don't know if I can hold out hope only to be told it's over. I'm not getting any younger, and that fight against Collins was my ticket out of here and into the big leagues."

"Look," he sits forward. "you're entitled to brew for a few days and mull it all over. But don't stew. You have people in your corner. People who love you and would do anything to see you succeed. You don't have to walk this road alone, D."

"What if I never heal?"

He shrugs his shoulder. "What if you do? You know what they say — it ain't over until that final bell rings."

With those final words of Kye's wisdom, he lifts himself out of the chair, leaving me to stew on my thoughts.

Should I allow myself to believe I can get through this injury and still come out on top?

God, I fuckin' hope so.

Gigantic Dick

DANNY

"Jesus Christ! Would you stop staring at the phone and just call her already?"

"Mind your own business."

"You're moping around my house. Therefore, it is my business."

I lift my crutch off the floor and swing it at Kye, clipping him in the shin.

"Fuck!" he cries out. "That hurt, asshole."

"Good."

He places his coffee on the table and glares at me.

"It's been four days, D. Do us both a favour and make the call."

I'm not proud of the way I spoke to Ava the other night, and I've spent every minute since she left feeling like The World's Biggest Asshole.

A title that, in my opinion, is well deserved.

I don't blame her for not reaching out. With the way I behaved, I deserve every millisecond of her silent treatment.

I should never have projected my shit on Avie, but with my new reality blindsiding me, I lost sight of what really matters. Her!

"If she wanted to talk to me, she would have called."

I fucked up, and I'm still trying to figure out how to fix it. It's not like I can rush over there with a big grand gesture. I can barely make it around Kye's house without having to sit down.

"Maybe she's just trying to give you the space you asked for."

I almost laugh at his ridiculous comment.

"Ava McCann wouldn't know what space was if it jumped up and slapped her. She is an in-your-face kind of girl. It's one of the reasons I love her."

"This is different, and you know it."

Could he be right? Could Ava be sitting around waiting for me to call?

No, I know her. If she wanted to talk to me, she would have shown up here and called me out for being such a gigantic dick. She's pissed and rightly-fucking-so.

My eyes flick back to my phone, checking it for the umpteenth time in the last ten minutes.

Kye pulls himself out of his recliner with a frustrated breath. "Well, you can't say I didn't try to talk some sense into your brainless head."

He plucks his keys off the table and heads for the door. "Call her, or don't, but for the love of Christ, figure it out before I get back from my training session. I can't bear another day of your lovesick crap."

The door clicks behind him, and I slump back into the couch, contemplating my next move.

I've already lost enough this week. I can't lose my girlfriend, too.

AVA

I HAVE HAD IT UP TO MY TIT'S WITH DANNY'S SILENT TREATMENT!

I don't care if his leg is hanging off. He is going to listen to me whether he wants to or not.

I march up Kye's driveway like the hounds of hell are nipping at my feet.

I'm so mad.

Mad that Danny got hurt.

Mad that he shut me out.

Mad at myself for letting him.

Four days I sat on my ass waiting for him to call, and four nights I went to bed disappointed that he didn't.

Nope, I am not allowing him to close down for one second longer.

Too aggressive? I think-fucking-not!

My fist greets the door with three loud knocks. "Danny O'Donoghue, you have twenty seconds to open this door. Or so help me, God! One," I start my countdown and make it to eighteen before the door swings open, showcasing a scorching, half-naked, tattooed man in sweatpants.

How is it he can rock those crutches like nobody's business?

Just look at him, standing there like a tall glass of water in the middle of a desert — dark hair pulled back into a sexy man bun, hot bulging muscles bare for me to lick. Who does he think he is, Jake Gyllenhall?

Stop staring. You're supposed to be mad at him, remember?

"Hey, Avie!"

"You!" I poke him in the chest. "Don't you dare, *'Hey, Avie,'* me!"

His eyes shoot open, wide like saucers. I waltz past him, walking my determined butt into the centre of the living room. The door clicks behind me, and I wait while he hobbles over to the couch.

"I was going to—"

I hold my hand up, cutting him off. "Sit!"

He lowers himself onto the couch, and I bend down and help him elevate his leg. Once I get him sorted, I stand up straight and draw in a frustrated breath.

"Look, D. I can't even begin to imagine how you must feel, and I won't stand here and pretend that I do. But I love you. And I will not let you push me away. Before I was your girlfriend, I was your friend, and friends show up. They are there for each other when times are tough. I'm not going to lie to you and tell you this is going to be an easy road, but will I fuck let you throw everything you've spent your life working on away because you're too scared to change the outcome? Hell no, I won't. So, starting right now —" I stomp my foot like a petulant child "—you're going to stop feeling sorry for yourself and become the goddamn fighter I know you are. Life's not about how hard of a hit you can give. It's about how many you can take and still keep moving forward."

Laughter dances around his eyes, then finally, it erupts from his lips. "Did you just quote Rocky Balboa?"

"You bet your ass I did!"

"Fuck, I love you."

Excuse me, what did he just say?

Using his crutches, he pulls himself off the couch and stands to face me. His eyes bore into mine, reflecting love and adoration. "Avie?"

"Yes!"

"If you had let me speak, you would have heard that I was about to call you before you stormed in here with a raging fire lit underneath your gorgeous ass."

"I—"

He lifts his finger to my lips, silencing me.

"It's my turn, now. And you're going to keep those sassy lips closed until I say what I need to say."

I nod, swallowing my tongue in the process.

"I'm so sorry for how I spoke to you. You didn't deserve my anger. You're the most important person in my life, and I couldn't stand you seeing me so low. So, I did the only thing I could think of — I pushed you away."

His hand caresses my cheek as he wipes the lone tear from beneath my eye with his thumb. "I understand that it was a dick move, and I'm sorry I upset you. I've had a few days to process my injury, and yes, it sucks, but it's not your fault. But you are right. I am not ready to give up the fight just yet. My time in the octagon isn't over. I need to fight, Avie, but I need you in my corner more."

I cover his hands with mine. "You have me, D. I am not going anywhere. We'll get through this, I promise you."

"It won't be easy, babe. I have a long road ahead of me. With the surgery and months of physical therapy. I'll be at the gym every chance I get."

"Then it's a good thing I have a new salon to keep me busy."

His smile is blinding. "You got the loan?"

"I got the loan."

His lips crash against mine, and everything else fades away.

He pulls away and kisses the tip of my nose.

"I love you, Avie."

I curl my lips into a cheeky smile. "And so you should. I'm pretty fucking awesome."

The Final Bell

DANNY

TWO YEARS LATER

THE FLOODLIGHTS DIM, AND THE ARENA FADES TO black.

The piercing roar of seventeen thousand people explodes around the MGM Grand, filling the darkness with electric energy that courses through my bones.

Dropkick Murphy blares through the surround

sound, letting America know that the Irish have arrived.

Las Vegas, baby! We made it.

I emerge from the tunnels with the strength of my team behind me. My face is projected on the four screens hovering above the octagon as the glow of green, white, and gold lights up the rafters.

This is it, the moment I spent my life preparing for — my first UFC title fight.

I reach the octagon and climb into the cage, and the cheers of the Irish fan's grow louder. I look out, dazed by the sea of tri-colour flags.

Two years ago, I tore my ACL, and I thought this dream was unreachable. But here I am, better than I have ever been, and more than ready to bring the title home.

I climb up the side of the cage and rest over the edge, my eyes searching ringside for the one woman who believed in me more than life itself.

My eyes lock on my wife, Ava O'Donoghue.

She looks fucking radiant in her skin-tight pale pink dress, her crazy pink and blue hair hanging in loose waves over her shoulders.

She lifts her hand to her mouth and blows me a kiss. "You got this, D." She yells over the fans.

All through my recovery, that woman stayed by

my side, cheering me on, pushing me forward, believing in me every step of the way.

The music shifts, changing to my opponent's theme song. Rian Collins — the current featherweight champion of the world.

He enters the cage, and our stand-off begins.

"Are you ready to get your ass handed to you... again?" His smirk curls on the corner of his mouth.

I step into his space. "This is my time. You better not be too attached to that belt, Collins, because I'm about to take it off you."

The referee breaks us apart, pushing us into our corners. I bounce on my feet, ready to finish the fight of my life.

In three, two, one.

Rian rushes forward, striking out with long, looping combinations. I shift right, dodging his over handed left.

"Do it, D!" Kye roars from behind the blue corner.

I wait, avoiding every throw. Rian kicks out, and I grip his ankle. He stumbles, and I take my chance. As I drop his leg, my head ducks to the left. I hit him with a triple threat — power, speed, and accuracy. My straight left connects to the soft spot on his jaw. And lights-fucking-out.

"Ladies and gentlemen, the referee has called a stop to this contest at fifty-two seconds of the very first round," the fight announcers voice booms into the microphone. "Declaring the winner by KNOCK-OUT. The new, undisputed UFC featherweight champion of the world, THE DOMINATOR, DANNY O'DON-O-GHUE!"

My family rushes into the cage, surrounding me while I kneel in disbelief. The crowd is wild, singing songs and chanting my name.

Before I know it, I'm on my feet, and there's a microphone shoved under my nose.

"Danny, how does it feel to be the new feather-weight champion of the UFC?"

I shake my head, trying to find the words to describe the feeling coursing through my veins. "Incredible. Absolutely incredible."

My eyes search the octagon until they land on my best friend. Drawing her closer with my eyes, she comes running and jumps into my awaiting arms. "OH MY GOD! YOU DID IT!"

Her lips brush against every inch of my face as she peppers me with a thousand kisses. "I'm so proud of you."

Gently, I place her onto her feet and kneel before her, underneath the watchful eye of the crowd. I grip her hips and pull her closer. Resting my head against her stomach, I whisper. "Did you hear that, princess? Daddy is a champ!"

HOURS OF PRESS CONFERENCES AND AN AFTER-PARTY to end all parties, later, we finally make it back to our penthouse suite.

"Put me down," Ava squeals as I sweep her off her feet and carry her over the threshold, bridal style. "I need to check-in with Charlie and make sure the salon is okay."

"Not happening, sweetheart. You've been so busy since you opened last spring. You're entitled to a few days break. I'm sure everyone can manage without you for a few more hours, Charlie included."

Waltzing into the room with my stunning wife in my arms, I only have one destination in mind — the bed. I lower her down onto the plush Egyptian cotton sheets and gaze down at how perfect she looks — her vibrant hair splayed across the white linen, and her cheeks blushed with a pretty shade of pink. "How the fuck did I get so lucky?"

She winks, sending shockwaves of desire straight to the head of my dick.

I drop to the floor, and one by one, I remove her shoes, then kiss my way up her left leg. "Avie, I've been thinking about fucking you all night, and now that I finally have you alone, I'm going to do just that."

My hand disappears under the short material of her dress, roaming over the edge of her thong. Curling my fingers, I take hold of the lacey material, then ever so fucking slowly, I peel them off. "Now, what were you saying about calling Charlie to see how she's coping with all the clients from Shear Lock Combs," I tease.

"Who?"

"That's what I thought."

Lowering my head, I run my tongue along her inner thigh. "How does it feel, Avie? Knowing the champion of the world is seconds away from fucking you into next week."

"You talk a big game, Danny Boy, but I've yet to see some action."

Her hand grips my hair, guiding me to where she needs me most.

"Fuck, Avie," I murmur against her clit as my fingertips grip her hips. I slide my tongue over every inch of her pussy, loving the way she moans with every brush, nip, and suck. Grinding her hips, she fucks my tongue, desperate for release.

"I need more," she cries out.

I stand, ripping my shirt over my head in one swift motion. I undo the button of my suit pants, and command, "On your knees, Ava."

She flips over, raising her ass into the air. I grip her hips and pull her to the edge of the bed, then sink so far into her depths I see fucking stars.

With each thrust, I feel her tightening around me.

My breaths become quicker.

Her hands grip the sheets, crumpling the fabric.

Our moans grow louder.

So goddamn good.

Needing to see her, I pull out. "Let me see you, baby."

She rolls onto her back, and I position myself at her entrance, slowly running the head of my dick across her slit before finally pushing forward.

"Oh, fuck. Yes!" A moan tumbles out of her mouth as I grind my hips, hitting the spot I know drives her crazy.

"There, Danny. Right there."

I groan as she tightens around me, and together we fall apart.

Rolling onto my side, I pull her into my chest and press my lips against her forehead.

We spend the rest of the night tangled up in each other as I hold her close, never wanting to let her go — my life, my love, and most importantly, my best friend.

Acknowledgements

Andrew, everyday with you is "living the dream".

Joshua and Benjamin, always remember Mammy loves you to the moon and back. Never forget how special you both are. Make sure you live life to its fullest potential. You are magic — don't let anyone tell you any different.

Shout out to the MIL, Liz, thanks for watching the boys when I was bogged down with deadlines. You held down the fort, picked up the slack, and made sure me and my hellions were fed.

To my wild at heart mother, thank you for showing me that without struggle, we can never truly be strong. For teaching me to never let anyone dim my sparkle; and that the "f word" is not a curse but a sentence enhancer. Love your favourite child.

To my siblings, Paul, Tony, Emma, David, and Aisling, I love you all. Thanks for supporting me on this crazy ride. Sorry if I became a hermit, ignoring all your calls. I promise to answer now. (Kidding, the next book won't write itself)

Danielle Paul, once again you played a stormer, cheering me on, and whipping me back into shape when I felt like giving up. You are a gem, and I'm so glad I met you (virtually). One day, we will have cocktails, and not over Instagram.

My ARC readers, thanks so much for everything you do for me, from the reviews to the AWESOME edits and social media posts. You the real MVPs of what I do. Stay AWESOME! Also, a big thank you to all the bloggers and readers who took the time to read this book. I appreciate it so much. Please leave a review on any (or if you're feeling generous) all of my social media platforms.

Much Love

Shauna

About the Author

Shauna lives in the small town land of Oldtown, North County Dublin; with her partner and her two little boys.

She always loved to read, to escape reality between the pages of a good book.

Her other hobbies include singing, art, all things spiritual, songwriting and binge-ing on Netflix series.

She believes we all have a little light inside us, but it's up to us to let it shine.

Also by Shauna McDonnell

THE 4CLOVER SERIES

LUCK, 4CLOVER BOOK ONE (CIAN) AVAILABLE NOW

LOVE, 4CLOVER BOOK TWO (CILLIAN) AVAILABLE NOW

FAITH, 4CLOVER BOOK THREE (CIARAN) AVAILABLE NOW

HOPE, 4CLOVER (CONOR) COMING MAY 2021
PRE-ORDER NOW!

Enjoyed WHAT IF IT'S YOU? Make sure you stay in the loop with UPCOMING BOOKS by following me on Instagram!

@shaunamcdonnellauthor

KEEP READING FOR A SNIPPET OF LUCK, 4CLOVER BOOK 1

CPSIA information can be obtained
at www.ICGtesting.com
Printed in the USA
LVHW052113180421
684849LV00023B/1743